NOT THE ONE

TONI ALEO

Editing by: Lisa Hollett of Silently Correcting Your Grammar

Cover Design: *Jay Aheer* *Simply Defined Art*

❀ Created with Vellum

To whiskey. You always seem like such a good idea.
At the time...

BEFORE YOU GET STARTED!

Why don't you join my newsletter for all the awesome and fun stuff I send out!
Sign up in confidence, NO SPAM EVER!

JOIN NOW!

PROLOGUE

Blue lights were flashing like mad, giving her a headache as she leaned against the police car.

Genevieve's body was shaking with fear, but a little bit of excitement was also bubbling deep inside of her. She knew damn well her family was going to flip. Once word got back to the country club, everyone would be talking about how the precious Genevieve Stone, daughter of the prestigious Murray Stone of Stone Masons, was caught trafficking drugs. The disappointment would ring loud in her father's voice—he'd probably take her credit card away. And her poor mother would probably wring her hands, steeling her nerves with a healthy dose of vodka in her morning juice.

Too bad Gen didn't care.

This trip was supposed to be the time of her life. She was going to see the world, but he'd said they had to stop back in his hometown first. What she didn't know was that he had been planning to bring a whole bunch of drugs back for his buddies to sell down in Lexington. When she found out, by opening the trunk to put her bag in, the smart part of her brain told her to run the other way.

But then he looked at her, his blazing blue eyes burning into hers as her lips pressed together in an "oh shit" kind of look. She should have taken that as a sign even he knew he was doing wrong, yet she just shrugged, threw her bag in, and went to the front seat.

She wasn't sure what she was doing, but she knew she wanted to go on this trip with him.

But after only three days in his hometown of Spring Grove, where she fell in love with small-town life and learned more about herself than she had in her whole life, Gen found herself leaning against a cop car with her hands cuffed behind her back.

Well, shit.

Terms were being thrown around—some she knew, some she didn't. But as she watched two cops from a neighboring town investigate, since Spring Grove only had one sheriff and a deputy, she knew she was in deep shit.

"I never thought I'd find you this hot with blue lights flashing on your skin, but I do."

Gen looked up, her eyes meeting his extra blue eyes since the lights were flashing directly into them. "Yeah, neither did I."

His lips pulled up at the side. "Probably should have stayed at home. Maybe my big brother would have taken you to the formal."

She scoffed. "Pfft. Like I wanted to go anyway."

"You did. You're made for that life."

She laughed, shaking her head. That was the furthest from the truth. She was actually more trailer park trash, like her mom used to be before her father found her and settled her in at the country club with diamonds hanging off her. "You must not know me."

"Not as well as I want," he said, making her heart flutter. He had that power, the one that made her whole body feel like it was tingling. Her mother said it was because she was young and naïve, but she was convinced it was just him. Theo. His thick shoulders, his darker than night hair. It was such a contrast, his eyes to his hair, and she loved it. She did. Even now, as she stood cuffed, knowing that serious charges could be coming her way, she still found him alluring. "But I know that formal would have been better than this."

She shrugged, looking away. "Says you."

He grinned over at her, and she met his grin with a smile. Things were easy between them. Since Gen had struggled her whole life, she enjoyed being with someone and not having to try so hard. She didn't have to be proper; she didn't have to make sure she had her manners turned on. She could just be her, burp if she wanted, and he would burp along with her. He was everything she had never experienced, and she couldn't get enough.

"Man, this sucks."

"Surely it's not a big deal. It's not like you're selling the stuff."

"I'm moving it, though," he confessed, shaking his head. "I just wanted to get my mom out of here."

Gen smiled. "She doesn't want to leave."

He laughed. "Yeah, but maybe I could have given her a better life than working in the damn diner."

"She loves the diner, though," she tried, but he wasn't listening. "It's all over with anyway. We were caught—"

"No, listen—" She looked up, her heart still in her throat as his eyes held hers. "I'm taking all the blame. Those are my drugs. I didn't tell you about them, okay?"

Her brows pulled together. "But I knew."

"Gen, really. This is going to be bad. You aren't this girl. The one that goes to jail for drugs—or anything else for that matter. Just trust me. Keep your mouth shut. Don't even talk to them."

"But—"

"No but, Gen. I'm this guy. You're not. This has been fun, but you gotta trust me. Let me take the fall. You act oblivious to everything, okay?"

"Theo—"

"For real, Gen. Okay? You know I love you, right?"

Her heart sang for him. "Yes, I love you too, but let me—"

"Darling, I'm not the one for you. You deserve the world. And this right here is a godsend, I promise. I do love you, Gen."

Before she could say anything else, the cops were closing in on them. And as she stood there, tears in her eyes, she knew she'd never see Theo Hudson again.

CHAPTER 1

Wrapping her hair around his fist, he yanked her head back, and her gaze met his in a hot and wanton embrace. *"Say it."*

She couldn't breathe or talk as she gazed up at him, whimpering. He loved it. He craved it. Her fear, it was a drug. "Who am I? Say it, Ash. Say who I am."

His voice was strained, his body shaking as his cock throbbed so deep inside of her. He almost couldn't think. Almost. He didn't know what was happening, he didn't understand what his body was doing, but he felt it deep in his soul, the need to bury himself inside of her and never leave.

She was his.

"Ash, say it," he demanded once more, squeezing a fistful of hair and causing her to cry out. It drove him mad, her body shaking against his, her eyes hooded as he looked down the pebbles of her spine to her round ass and small waist. God, he wanted to ruin her for every single man. She was his, damn it! "Now!"

"Daddy," she cried out, her body squeezing his as his toes curled into the carpet of her apartment. "Daddy... Please fuck me, Daddy."

His cock throbbed, his eyes squeezing shut as his fist tightened and his hand gripped her. He was about to explode—

Genevieve Stone jumped when her headphones were knocked

off her head, Lady Gaga crooning from where they'd landed in her lap before her eyes quickly narrowed. Slamming her laptop shut in frustration, she glanced up and complained, "What the hell?"

Her fiancé, Montgomery, looked down at her, annoyance on his beautiful face as he shook his head. His eyes were narrowed, his full lips pressed together on a face free of hair, looking so clean and tidy as always. But that didn't stop the expression of pure displeasure on his face. He was wearing a very expensive looking pair of blue slacks and pressed button-up shirt that matched the greenish blue of his eyes. The blue suit jacket was unbuttoned and hung open as he pressed his hands to his hips. "I've been calling up to you."

She glared before placing her headphones on top of her laptop. "I'm working, and you know I always have my sound-canceling headphones on when I'm working. You bought them for me."

He didn't seem pleased, but really, he never was. This wasn't the first time he'd found himself at the bottom of the stairs yelling for her, only to trek upstairs to find her in her zone. Writing her heart out. Not that she cared about his inconvenience; she was working. He knew that. "I understand, but you were also aware that our mothers were coming today for wedding planning. They're here. Waiting."

She rolled her eyes, letting her head fall back as she groaned. She had forgotten they were coming. "Mont, please, I'm in the zone. Distract them."

He didn't seem to care or have any intentions of distracting his insane mother. Her mother would be just fine sitting down at the table, looking through magazines while she waited. She understood Genevieve's career. She supported her. "We're getting married in a little over a month. Your book can wait."

She tried not to scream. "I'm on a deadline."

"Which I told you to cancel because of the wedding."

"I don't make the deadlines, my publisher does."

He gave her a dismissive look. "I think they can make an

exception for you since you are getting married and there is plenty of smut in the world."

The fight bubbled inside of her, but she didn't have it in her today. Not when she had to deal with their mothers, and especially not as they'd had this fight at least once a week since deciding to get married. Yes, as awful as that sounded, they'd decided. They had been together for over five years, lived together for three of them. She loved him, she did. She was comfortable, they were happy, and things worked. He went to work, she stayed home and worked, and they had sex.

When they had time.

When he brought up that maybe they should get married, it seemed like a good idea. Of course, their families were over the moon since they had been asking the two of them to tie the knot for a while. At first, it all went so quickly that it really didn't seem as though anything had changed. They picked a date, she picked a dress, and things were still good. But then, Montgomery's mother had started to come over more. She wanted everything planned to a tee, and that's when Genevieve began to notice her own lack of patience with everything. She just wanted to get married and to go back to their normal, but it seemed like his mother was scratching at her nerves. Soon Genevieve found that she and Montgomery were at each other's throats more than they weren't. And more than they had ever been.

Things had always been effortless. But lately, they were not even close to easy. Nothing was good enough: her clothes, her weight, her hair. He always had something negative to say. And when it came to her writing, Montgomery wasn't supportive. Genevieve didn't understand it. He hadn't been like that before. He'd seemed to love her, but she didn't feel that way all the time now.

Especially when it came to her career.

It was mildly mind-blowing. She was extremely successful in the romance world as Zoe Jayne. She had hit all the bestselling lists, she had been featured all over the world, there were even talks for movies, but Montgomery didn't feel it was a career people could know about. According to their friends—and some of his family—she worked in insurance. Before it hadn't mattered, but as soon as he planned to marry her, they had to lie to all their new friends. Man, she hated hiding her career, but she loved him, and because of that, she respected his wishes.

Except when he pulled shit like this.

"I don't write just smut, Mont, and you know that," she complained, rolling her eyes. "Either way, I have to finish this. I only have three more weeks, and I'm not even halfway done."

He shrugged before heading for the door. "Our mothers are downstairs. Do you want me to send them up, or are you coming down?"

As she watched his retreating back, she felt her blood boil. "I want you to tell them to come back tomorrow."

But he didn't acknowledge her words. She even heard him say that she was on her way once he reached the stairs. She knew he was nervous about the wedding. Over three thousand people would be attending. Everyone from his architecture firm would be there, plus his whole extended family and hers. It was a production for sure, but she really needed to get this book done. Not only for her deadline but also for her characters. They were screaming to be written, and it was her job to do so. So why couldn't the man she was about to spend her life with understand that?

To Montgomery, her writing was just a hobby, not a career. He thought it was a joke. But to her, it was way more than a career. It was a part of her. She had to write, she had to give her characters life, and she'd be damned if anyone would hold her back. As a result, all Montgomery and Genevieve did was argue. How she was wasting her time. How the wedding was more important. He wanted her to quit, but she wouldn't, and she knew it drove him crazy. She didn't care.

And she sure as hell didn't care about this damn wedding.

Why couldn't they just elope? Go to Vegas or even the courthouse, she didn't care. She just wanted it over...after she finished her book. She hated the planning process of the wedding and, most of all, the arguing with Montgomery's mother, Verna. Verna was acting as if she were planning a wedding for the Prince of Wales, it was so pathetically lavish. Of course, Genevieve's mom was eating it up since she had grown up poor, marrying into money when she got pregnant with Gen. But it wasn't really Gen's jam. She liked low-key things, and when she expressed that, she was shot down by Verna and then Montgomery. They were about the extravagant and ostentatious. Gen just wanted somewhere to write and someone to love.

"Gen, honey!"

She groaned loudly at her mother's overly cheery voice. "Coming," she called out before reluctantly getting out of her office chair and heading out of the room, locking the door behind her. She was very weird when it came to her work in progress. Not that Montgomery ever showed interest in reading her stuff, but if he had, she'd make him wait. Still, though, she didn't want anyone seeing or reading her unfinished manuscript, so she always locked her office door.

Heading down the grand staircase and then cutting through the den of the very upscale home Montgomery had inherited when they were younger, Gen let out a long sigh. She couldn't wait to start decorating their home. Since they weren't married yet, Verna wouldn't let her do anything to the bachelor pad Montgomery's uncle had left him, and she was really sick of the feel of it. It was old and smelled of cigars. She swore it, though Montgomery said she was crazy and constantly agreed with his mother. He was a mama's boy to the extreme.

As she entered the large dining room where Verna and her mother sat with all the wedding crap known to man laid out on the table, she suppressed a groan when Montgomery stopped her by grabbing her waist and kissing her jaw. "Good luck."

She leaned into him. Though she was annoyed, she did love this man. Had for most of her adult life. While it hadn't been by choice, more expectations from her family at first, it wasn't like that any longer. He made her happy...when he was home and not calling her job stupid. "Yeah, thanks."

"Don't pout," he demanded, kissing her once more. "It will all be done soon."

She gave him a dry look as she shook her head. "I really need to work," she stressed once more.

Before he could comment, his mother was speaking, "Oh, Genevieve, your little book can wait. This is your wedding."

"That we shouldn't still be planning."

His mother didn't like that one bit as her own mother stood, reaching out for Gen's hand. "I have something to show you."

Before her mother could pull her away, Montgomery said, "I'll see you later."

"Are you working late?"

"Yeah."

Her shoulders fell. While on one hand, that meant his mother would take forever to leave. On the other, once she did, Gen would be able to work. But it meant Verna had to leave first. "Okay."

He squeezed her hip before heading out the door, the shoulders of his jacket taut against his wide chest and muscular back. He had gotten a haircut the day before, so his hair was perfectly trimmed, his neck so thick and so sexy that soon a grin pulled at her lips. They had both been so busy for the last couple months that sex hadn't been a thing that happened often, but realizing his hair was turning her on meant one thing. They needed to fuck.

ASAP.

Inhaling hard, she looked to her mother, ignoring the annoyed look on Verna's face as her mom pulled her to the end of the table where a box was sitting. "Mom, what is all this?"

Her mother's gray eyes sparkled as she squeezed Gen's hand. "Gen, love, I was going through the attic and found this box of your stuff. I had no clue what it was until I opened it and realized it was all your things from when you'd go and stay at Spring Grove."

Curiosity took over as she moved past her mother to the box.

She thought she had everything packed away up in her own attic, but apparently, that wasn't the case. On the top of all her things was a Polaroid of her laptop on a table with a beautiful lake behind it. Covering her mouth, Gen exhaled hard. "Wow. I took this when I finished, *Capture Me*, my first book."

Her mother beamed. "I know. I don't know how this got left behind."

"Sorry to bother you, but are we going to get started?"

Gen ignored Verna as she reached for another picture, this one of only the Blu, a B&B back in Spring Grove, Kentucky, with the tulips in bloom. Smiling, she moved through the contents of the box as chills ran down her back. The Blu was her favorite place in the world. When she was younger—and rebellious as hell—she had gone on a road trip. At the time, it was silly, and the trip was only supposed to be for a weekend, a last hurrah before college, but when they arrived in Spring Grove, she found herself at the Blu. So much had happened in the span of three days that before she knew it, she didn't leave for a month. Oh, everyone was so mad, but she didn't care. Especially when she wrote her first novel there.

Man, the memories.

"You haven't been in years."

She nodded, running her fingers along the tulips. "Four years. I bet the tulips are up."

"Oh, I'm sure."

A grin tickled her lips. "Man, I miss that place."

"You should go back."

She glanced over at her mother, laughing. "I can't. So much going on. My book...and the wedding."

Gen's gaze returned to the box as her mother thought for a moment. "Don't you have to have the book finished before the wedding?"

Gen nodded, looking up. "I do."

"So, go. Don't you think it would be amazing to finish your last novel as a single woman in the house where you wrote your first?"

Gen grinned at that. "Yeah, it would be awesome."

TONI ALEO

"I think it would be silly, and you're right, we have so much planning to do," Verna interjected. "We have a lot of work to do."

But her mother waved Verna off. "That we can handle, Verna, surely. She's so stressed."

Verna rolled her eyes. "She wouldn't be if she'd just quit this silly writing."

Gen's mother looked back at Verna and shook her head. "It's her dream, and I believe in her dreams. I will take more of the load. I'll text you if I need you. Go, my love, you need this."

But Genevieve just laughed. "I don't even know if they're still open! I haven't even seen anything about them. I don't know..." She shook her head. It was a crazy thought, an insane one, but she couldn't shake the feeling it was a great one. She wasn't sure if she should or even could. She knew she would definitely finish the book. Every time she went to the Blu to write, her writing juices flowed like the Amazon, and it was almost magical. She loved that place, she did, but could she get away? Would Montgomery be okay with it?

Probably not.

"I'm sure my son would not appreciate his bride leaving weeks before their wedding."

Rolling her eyes, Genevieve tried to ignore Montgomery's mother, but her mother was glaring back at Verna. "I doubt Montgomery would even notice with how much he is working lately."

"Well, Fawn, he is very successful. He has to work."

"I never said he didn't," her mother countered. "But like your son, my daughter is extremely successful, and she needs to get away."

Verna rolled her eyes. "She can write anywhere."

Fawn glared. "While this may be true, why don't you look out for yours, and I'll look out for mine. She needs a getaway, just her. She's breaking out."

"Thanks, Mom." Genevieve glared as her mother ran her hands along her pimpled jaw. She was like a teenager going through puberty, but it always happened when she was stressed. She knew she was under pressure, but maybe it was more than usual.

Shit, maybe her mom was right.

Shooting her a forgiving smile, Fawn patted her hand. "Go."

But Genevieve still wasn't sure.

She wanted to. Lord, did she. She'd leave right that second, with nothing but her laptop and toothbrush, but she didn't. Instead, she replaced the pictures in the box and sat down to plan her wedding.

While she was sure her mother knew, Gen would never admit to Verna that she wasn't paying even the least bit of attention to the plans they were making.

Because her thoughts were captivated by all her memories of the Blu.

CHAPTER 2

When Gen heard the front door close downstairs, she turned off her music and swallowed hard as she shut the lid of her laptop. She hadn't planned on staying up and waiting for Montgomery to get home, but the more she'd thought about the Blu, the more she knew she had to go. It would be so great for her. Time to herself. Get away from his awful mother and the planning of this spectacle called a wedding. She needed this. For her sanity, at the very least.

Twirling her engagement ring on the desk, she watched as it spun, the light catching the over-the-top diamond she really didn't care for. She'd told Montgomery she didn't want such a huge diamond. She'd wanted a small one, something easy to type with but, of course, this damn diamond weighed more than a baby! Okay, that was an exaggeration, but still. It was heavy, and she hardly ever wore it.

Placing the ring in the little bowl she kept on her desk for it, she turned in her seat, pushing her hair up into a better bun as she listened to Montgomery move around the downstairs, probably putting away his keys, taking off his coat, and getting something to drink. He had a routine when he came home late at night. He usually settled down with a beer while watching the sports highlights. She was about to get up when she heard him coming up the stairs, which was a tad surprising. When he appeared in the doorway, his brows were raised.

"I thought I heard you up. I didn't expect you to be," he said, undoing the buttons on his wrists before shaking his sleeves out as he came toward her. "It's almost midnight."

She nodded, crossing her legs. "Just working. Our mothers didn't leave until ten."

He made a face before rolling his eyes. He leaned down then, kissing the top of her head. "Yeah, my mother called." He cupped her chin. "You look exhausted."

Her brows pulled together as she nodded. "I am, but what did she want?"

He shook his head, running his hands through his hair before he tucked them into his pockets. "She wasn't very happy with your meeting. Asked me not to have your mother there—" Gen went to protest, but he held up his hand. "But I told her, no way, that your mother will be one hundred percent in this."

She smiled weakly. "Thank you."

His lips quirked a bit, showing a bit of the guy she had fallen for so long ago. It seemed like eons ago. She hadn't wanted to go out with him. She had grown up with him and wasn't the least bit attracted to him, but then her mother pushed and his mother pushed and she found herself at dinner with him. It was that quirky grin that got her. She found it endearing, and back then, when he wasn't stressed with work and they were having a lot more sex, she fell in love. Her smile grew a bit as she reached up, taking his hand. He was a good man, and she knew he would be supportive of her going to the Blu. He knew how much it meant to her.

Clearing his throat, he rolled his eyes once more. "She told me everything that was going on with the wedding, and then told me to remind you that you have a fitting this week."

Gen's brows pulled together, and she crossed her arms over her chest. "That doesn't make sense. I already had my fitting."

He shrugged. "She said she wanted it more formfitting, so she ordered a size down."

Gen's eyes widened as her stomach dropped. "Um, that won't work. I'm a size fourteen. Going down is a twelve. There is no way."

He shrugged. "She has full faith you'll be able to fit into it with the diet and all—"

She threw her hands up, anger vibrating her body. "Mont, I'm not on a diet! I haven't been. I told her I was to get her off my back. My dress is in the closet. I don't want another size. I'm fine!"

He held his hands up. "Then ignore it."

"Mont, that's bullshit. She wants me to be a fucking Barbie!"

He rolled his eyes. "But I don't," he said simply, taking her hips in his hands. "I love your shape. Could you lose some weight? Sure. But then, so could I."

She glared, moving out of his hands. "You think I need to lose weight?

He met her gaze, and she could see the realization of what he'd said. Shaking his head, he muttered, "Fuck, no. I'm sorry. That came out so wrong. I love you. I love you the way you are. I promise." Taking her face in his hands, he pressed his nose to hers. "Really, Gen, I'm sorry."

She bit into her lip, exhaling hard. "It's fine." But it wasn't. She was very confident in her body. She loved herself, but there was always that little bit of self-consciousness when it came to his mother. Verna always made her feel like a cow, and damn it, she wasn't. She was curvy and fucking beautiful, damn it.

"It isn't. I'm sorry."

She smiled, covering his hands with hers. "Okay." He moved his nose along hers, and her eyes drifted shut slowly, her heart thumping loudly in her chest. "I miss you."

He nodded. "I know, it's been crazy."

"It has." She cleared her throat. "Which I wanted to talk to you about."

He opened his eyes as he pulled back some. "Gen, you know I can't take off any time. I know you miss me—"

"No, I know that," she interjected, holding his gaze. "I want to go away and finish my book."

His brows pulled together. "What? Why?"

"Because I can't get anything done here. I'm distracted by you, when you are home, by our mothers, this wedding—which should be done and you know it. Even my mom said I should go away."

He shook his head. "I mean, yeah, but why? Why do you have to go away? I'll just tell my mom to let it go. Let the planners take over."

Her shoulders fell. "Mont, I'm not inspired here. Usually, my books flow, but I'm stuck. I need to go somewhere where I can get my writing juices flowing."

His brow furrowed as he gazed down at her. "So where are you trying to go?"

"The Blu."

He scoffed. "You want to go all the way to Spring Grove, Kentucky to write? That's a twelve-hour drive from here, or a two-hour drive from the nearest airport since they don't have a damn airport of their own."

"I know, but I write so well there."

He shook his head, crossing his arms over his chest. "Fine, you go, and then you're done when you finish." He didn't put it to her as a question; he almost demanded it, though she wasn't sure what the hell he was talking about.

She pulled her brows together as she shook her head. "I don't understand. Of course, I'll be done when I finish."

"No, I mean done, done. This 'career' will be over."

She laughed, her eyes widening. "Are you insane? No, no it won't."

"My mom thinks it's—"

"I don't give seven shits what your mother thinks of my career. It only matters what I think—"

"That's selfish! You have to worry about what I think."

"And I take that into consideration, I do, but this is who I am. You knew this before we ever got together. I am a writer."

"It's pointless."

"No, it's not!" she yelled back, her eyes wide and full of anger. "Mont, like your job is a part of you, my writing is a part of me."

"It's not a career."

She rolled her eyes. "Montgomery, I make six figures a year. Tell me that is not a successful career. Please. Tell me."

"It doesn't matter. You can't go out and tell people, I'm a smut writer."

"Yes, I can," she insisted, throwing her hands up. "It's not just smut, though. It's love. It's heartbreak, loss, vulnerability. It's life. I give my characters a life for people to get lost in. How dare you not understand this is a part of me. Do you not know me?"

He shook his head. "Of course I do, Gen. I just hate that part of you. It's silly to me."

She glared, her heart aching in her chest. "Montgomery, do you know how that hurts me?" Her eyes burned into his, but he showed no remorse. "I have no clue what you do. I have no need to know because, no matter what, I support you because I love you. Unlike other women would, I don't question your late nights, your meetings, nothing—because I trust you and I support you. I know for a fact you're working hard for us, for our future. Don't you realize I'm doing the same? That my career will be able to put our children through college?"

He rolled his eyes. "We don't need it."

"But I do," she said simply. "I need this outlet."

"If you'd get a normal job—"

She rolled her eyes. "No. I won't."

"Genevieve."

"Mont." She held his heated gaze, inhaling hard as she shook her head. "This is who I am. This is who you're marrying. I'm not quitting. I'm not stopping. I'm going to the Blu, where I'll write this novel—"

"I'm pretty sure I've made it clear I don't want you to go."

She glared up at him. "No, you said, I go, I quit after I'm done. Which I told you, no, I'm not."

He glared back. "Fine. I don't want you to go."

Her blood boiled. "Okay. Why?"

"Because we're getting married in a matter of weeks!"

"And I'll be back in time—"

"We have parties to attend the next three weeks."

"And you can go stag, say I'm away."

"Gen, this is ridiculous."

She laughed as it all dawned on her. "You know what I think is ridiculous, Mont? The fact that I'm just now realizing you have no intention of accepting my career. I think, for the longest time, I was trying to convince myself that one day you would. That you'd be supportive once we were married, but now I know that's not true."

"It's not a real career!"

"It is to me," she answered back, shaking her head. "But, Montgomery, I'm not walking down that aisle if you can't accept me for who I am. I am an author. It is who I am. Just like the chip in my front tooth or the stretch marks on my hips or even the curves that you love. It is all a part of me." Clearing her throat free of the emotion that was threatening to choke her, she looked down at the ground. "We've danced around this for years, and I can't anymore, Mont. I won't do this if you can't accept me."

"So you're calling off the wedding?"

She looked up, a serious expression on her face. "Do you want that?"

"No." His gaze was wild as it bored into hers. "I want you to quit, be a regular housewife."

"It's not in my makeup, never has it been. When I look at my future, I see a baby on my boob as I work. Or one in a wrap on my back while I map out my stories. There isn't a moment in my future where I don't see myself writing."

He just shook his head, looking away. "This is all insane."

"It is. It's a fight we don't need to have if you'd just accept it."

"Or you can just quit."

"Not happening."

Their gazes locked, anguished, as she cleared her throat. Her heart was pounding, and her chest hurt. She knew he didn't do ultimatums, but she wouldn't back down on this. She wasn't the kind of girl to change herself for a man. She hadn't before Montgomery, and she wouldn't now. She loved him, she did, but she'd be damned if he wouldn't accept her as she was. "Use these two weeks to figure out what you want, Montgomery. I'll have my phone."

He snorted loudly in disbelief. "Just like that."

"Just like that."

Turning on his heel, he left the room in a huff. What she hated most was that she wanted to chase him, ask him to support her and believe in her.

But she didn't, because he wasn't chasing her.

CHAPTER 3

H e wasn't good enough for her. He knew that, staring deep into her brown gaze that was drowning in tears. He couldn't be the man she needed. The man she deserved. He wasn't that guy.

"Don't leave, Travis. Please."

"Ash, I'm not good."

"You are," she stressed, pressing her hands into his chest. "I know you are."

"I'm the furthest from a good man. I've cheated, I've stolen. Ash, I've fucking killed."

Horror filled her face as she shook her head. Yes, all that was in his past, but still, it shaped him into society's version of the piece of shit who was standing before her. But she didn't look at him like that. She looked at him like he was worthy of love from an angel. "Not on purpose."

"It was my fault. I was drunk, I got into the fight that killed him. I'm junk, baby. Run away."

She shook her head. "No. I can't."

"You have to."

"I won't."

"Ashley..."

"Travis, I love you."

His eyes fell shut as he inhaled deeply, his whole body moving with the action. He knew she loved him. He knew he should have stepped away after the first time he got her in his arms, but he couldn't. He craved her. Needed her. But he couldn't ruin her life the way he had ruined his. He cared for her too much.

Shit, he might even love her.

Fuck.

When he looked up, to tell her to leave him, and fast, she was undressing. His eyes widened as he choked out, "Ashley?"

"Take me, Travis," she said, her eyes burning into his as she skimmed out of her panties. "Against this table. I want every single inch of you inside me. Make my body ache, not my heart."

He was speechless as his sweet, beautiful angel leaned on the table, perking her ass in the air. His cock throbbed, straining against his shorts, as he watched the inside of her appear, her slick center glistening at him. Screaming for him. Just like her eyes were.

"Take me," she whispered, looking over her shoulder at him. "Now."

His hands shook, his heart pounding but he—

"When is your flight?"

Gen jumped as she shut her computer, and she inhaled quickly at the sound of Montgomery's voice. They hadn't spoken since their fight two nights before. He was working, she was working, and she was pretty sure they were both ignoring his mother. Which she actually had no problem with whatsoever.

"My car should be here in about ten."

"Oh. I thought I was driving you."

Still not looking at him, she picked at her nails. "I assumed you'd be at work."

"I took off to take you."

"Well, you should have said something."

She looked back at him. He was wearing a pair of shorts and a button-down shirt. Very casual but also very sexy. She was so used to seeing him in either a suit or naked that seeing him in the clothes he used to wear before he became a workaholic sort of made butterflies go crazy in her stomach. "You should dress like that more often," she said before she could stop herself.

His brows pulled together as he shrugged. "I'm always working."

"Which is a problem."

His brows furrowed more. "You've never complained before."

"Because you were living your dreams," she said, standing and reaching for her laptop bag. "I supported you."

He didn't say anything as she put everything in her bag and then put it on her shoulder before pulling down the cuffs of her shorts. Looking up at him, she exhaled. "My car should be here in a few."

Before she could pass, though, he held up a hand to her. "Gen, stop."

"What?" she asked, looking up into his heated blue-green gaze. She could see the hurt, the uncertainty, but she couldn't back down on this. If it came down to him or her writing, she was choosing her writing. She could never be happy as just a housewife.

"Genevieve, it feels like you are calling this off."

Did it?

She shook her head. "I don't want to."

"Then don't."

"I won't," she stressed, gazing up at him. "But I won't stop writing. I won't stop giving life to my characters or publishing. Not only do I love it, but I have to do that. You knew that, surely you knew that going in."

"I didn't think this was a forever thing."

"Well, it is."

"But—"

She held her hand up. "I'm not quitting, and I want to be with you. I love you. But I will not be with you when you won't support me."

"That's not fair. That's basically an ultimatum and only weeks before the wedding. That's fucked up, Gen."

She nodded. "You're absolutely right. This should have happened years ago, so both of us wouldn't be standing here, staring into each other's faces, thinking, 'Fuck, we just wasted years on each other—'"

"I don't feel I've wasted anything. I want to be with you."

"And I want to be with you, I do, Mont. I love you, but I refuse to stop what I love. Why can't I have you and my career?"

He threw his hands up, frustration filling his features. "Because it's stupid. It isn't even a real career. It's like painting, no one makes a career of art. It's dumb—"

She laughed ruefully. "And that's where you are wrong, and I'm sorry, but basically a snob because there are plenty of people who make a career from art, from dance, from singing. Anything. People love people who are creative. It's a passion—"

"It's an excuse to be lazy."

She inhaled sharply, her eyes widening, completely taken aback by that. "When have I ever been lazy? Please, tell me a time."

"You sit up in that room—"

"And I work, I clean, I come to your events, I even bring you lunch if you ask. I have done everything but stop writing. That's not fair to say. I am not lazy. Creative people are not lazy. They are geniuses, if anything. For goodness' sake, Mont, you design buildings. You're basically creative."

He recoiled in horror. "No. I'm a developer."

"Which is the same fucking thing!" she yelled, striking her hips. "Same thing."

Before he could go on, a horn sounded and then the doorbell. She shook her head as he looked away, both of them breathing hard. "I have to go."

"I don't think you should go."

"Well, I'm sorry," she said, reaching for her bags. "But I don't care. The same way you don't care about my career."

He glared back at her. "We have a lot to discuss."

"No, Mont, we've said enough. I know damn well all we'll do is go round and round the same issue," she said, moving past him and into the hall. She couldn't believe everything had blown up in her face like this. She thought she'd had it all. The man, the career, the life, but she was obviously ignoring the big fat elephant that had the potential to crash their so-called perfect life. "Take these two weeks to think this over. Hell, to miss me and to want to accept my career. I don't know. But I'm not doing this," she said, moving her hand between them, "if you can't support me. So when I come home in two weeks, it'll be to pack my shit or get married."

"This is ridiculous," he muttered as the horn beeped again. "We need to fix this."

"Can we?" she asked, holding his gaze. "I'm ready. You're the one who's not accepting me."

"Gen, this is stupid—"

"Yeah, we're done here." With that, she turned and started down the hall, shaking her head. Tears stung her eyes. She couldn't believe this. All she wanted to do was finish her book. Yeah, she didn't want this huge wedding, but damn it, she did love him.

"What is this? You getting cold feet? Need a last hurrah?"

She rolled her eyes. Looking back at him, she said, "I'm going to go finish my book, not go to Vegas."

"But you're going to the place where he was—"

She laughed, shaking her head. "Are you serious?"

He shrugged, looking away. "It just seems fishy."

"I have not seen or heard from him in years. Swallow your issues with your daddy's affairs when it comes to me. Because I'm not him. I don't cheat. I have never given you any kind of reason to assume that. Let's remember, I'm not the one who stepped out on the other."

It was a low blow, but she couldn't help it. Eyes flashing with anger, he yelled back, "We buried that. I was drunk, it was one time. Don't bring it up."

"Don't accuse me of something I have no intention of doing."

He scoffed. "But, Gen, is it cheating when you're separated?"

"Hell, I don't know, and I sure as hell don't want to find out."

"Sure, you don't."

The horn beeped once more, and not even the sound could

prompt her to shut her mouth as it hung open in complete shock. How dare he? She had never in their relationship done anything but love and support him. She'd never step out on him, and damn it, she took him back when he did it to her. This was bullshit. Straight bullshit.

Shaking her head, she turned, heading for the stairs. "It's as if you don't even know me."

"Maybe I don't," he called after her.

That was when the tears started to fall.

That was also the moment she realized she might have just wasted five years of her life.

CHAPTER 4

Swimming her hand through the air as she drove, Gen felt the sun warm her face.

She was here. Spring Grove, Kentucky.

Well, she had about fifteen minutes until she entered town, but a grin was already on her face. Gen had decided to leave her issues and problems with Montgomery back at the airport where she had landed. Once she picked up her car, threw the top down, and got in, she found herself singing and basking in the heat of the beautiful sun that was setting over Kentucky Lake. The whole flight to Kentucky, all she did was replay their arguments. Even the one they'd had two nights ago. She really didn't understand how the hell she hadn't noticed that not once had he told her he loved her. It hurt her, but she wouldn't let the tears fall anymore.

Not when she was in her magical place to finish her book.

She knew she had a lot to think about. If Montgomery didn't accept her career, what in the world would she do? But then, did she even want to be with someone who obviously didn't want to be with her as she was? Lord, how did this happen? Thankfully, they hadn't merged their accounts yet. They had been planning on it, but he had been so busy. Like always. But would she stay in DC? Would she move back to New York where she went to college?

Yelling out, she shook her head. "No, you are not doing this now. You will figure it out once you go back home and see if your so-called boyfriend is gonna get his stupid head out of his ass and support you—or better yet, love you."

But even saying the words out loud, she couldn't help but have no faith in them. Montgomery hadn't supported her ever, but now he was vocal about it. They had never discussed their problems; they just decided to get married. "And then everything went to shit," she muttered to herself, her long, golden-brown hair blowing in the wind. It didn't matter, though. None of it. She was going to write Travis and Ashley's story, and she'd send it off to her publisher. Then she'd figure out her life.

When the tears threatened to fall once more, she took a calming breath. She had this. But man, he pissed her off so damn bad. How in the world did he think it was okay to accuse her of leaving to cheat on him? She'd never do that! It just didn't make sense; it was almost like he wanted her to leave him. To call off everything. Or maybe she was just projecting.

Damn it, he made her so fudging mad.

And confused.

She didn't want to be confused on this; she wanted to know one way or another. They loved each other, and they were going to spend the rest of their days together. But she didn't truly feel that. She felt uncertainty. Confusion. And she hated it. Damn it, she was crying again. Wiping her face, she shook her head before turning up the music so loud that she couldn't think. All she could do was sing along with Sam Hunt about a back road, one she was probably driving on.

Because the road into Spring Grove wasn't like others. It wasn't a highway or even a main road. It was almost a dirt road, but nicer since it was paved, though with no lines. If someone came toward her, she would need to pull over, but she hadn't run into that problem yet. The trees were like she remembered, so bright green and blanketing the road with shade. They clouded the road to the point where she couldn't see anything but the light at the end of it, which would be the entrance to Spring Grove. She remembered the first time she'd driven this stretch.

She had been scared shitless.

She was newly eighteen, and her phone wouldn't stop ringing. Her parents were livid that she had run off with him, but she just wanted to feel something. She wanted to have fun. Be rebellious. She wanted to piss everyone off, and boy, had she. A grin pulled at her lips as she shook her head, thinking of how young and stupid they were. Well, he wasn't, he was three years older, and he was complete trouble.

But man, was he fun.

Theo.

She hadn't seen or heard from him in over ten years. Not that she had been keeping up with the time, but when he did climb into her thoughts, she couldn't help but grin. She should hate him, but how could she when he gave her the best two weeks of her life? Even with the cops throwing her in jail and everything else that had happened, she would almost always think of her time with him as a blast. He brought her to Spring Grove, he gave her this magical place, and she would always be thankful for that.

She swallowed hard as she drove down the long road. Her mind wandered where it shouldn't. She pondered where he was. Was he still in jail? Was he out doing his thing? A chill ran through her when she thought that he could be here with his mom. She knew his mom lived in Spring Grove, since the topic of Montgomery's father's whore was almost always brought up when Verna was drinking. It was the scandal of the country club.

Bruce Hudson's second life with another woman and another son.

Oh, man, it was nasty when it went through the country club when Gen was seventeen. Theo had been brought in to be raised right and not by a whore, but he, of course, resisted and stole from his father's other family. He was treated like a pariah by basically everyone but Gen. She found him intriguing and wanted nothing more than to be found making out with the bad boy of the country club. Oh, how it pissed off her family. The love affair between them was quick, mind-blowing, and exhilarating, but then he convinced her to leave with him, and well, things went downhill fast.

Even so, they were the best moments of her life.

When the trees opened out in front of her, she saw a sign in the shape of a barrel that read:

Welcome to Spring Grove.
Home of the McElroy Distillery.
Pop: 567

She was here.

A certain kind of giddiness filled her as she drove into the heart of the small town. Smacking her hands to the steering wheel as she sang along to the radio, she had a smile on her face. That was, until she noticed she forgot her engagement ring.

"Shit, he's gonna kill me," she muttered as she turned onto the main road of the town. The town square circled a huge fountain made up of barrels on top of barrels, with water coming out of all the ends, and cement statues of little children playing among them. All the necessities of the town surrounded it. The post office, the police department, the court, the fire department, the clinic, everything was right there, making a huge ring around the fountain. As she drove around the square, she ended up on the main street where all the businesses were located. When she looked up on the hill, she saw McElroy Distillery, which was the tourist attraction for the small town. They made the best whiskey in her opinion, which was also the opinion of the rest of the town. It still looked huge and glorious with the sun setting behind it. It was breathtaking. Nothing had changed, Gen decided as she drove, and that made her unbelievably happy. In DC, everything changed, daily, but here, it was like time stood still.

The Blu was on the outskirts of town, at the bottom of the hill the distillery was on. Also at the bottom of the hill was the town church. She would sit outside the B&B on Sunday mornings, watching as everyone came in, before the beautiful hymns would fill the back patio of the Blu. She loved it, and even though the owner, Ms. Neil, would beg Gen to come to church with her, she wouldn't. It wasn't her home church, and she didn't want to be an imposter. Everyone knew everyone in Spring Grove, and the tourists were the outsiders.

But Gen always felt like she was at home.

Rolling through town, she took in all the people walking around and doing what small-town folks did. She couldn't wait to get some downtime and explore. But first, she had to check in and get some words down. That was crucial. She was already off her schedule with her traveling.

Going out of town, she drove for about ten minutes before she reached the Blu. She inhaled gratefully as she took in the beauty of her magical place. It stood in all its glory, and she was pleased to see it hadn't changed. It was a Victorian style house with a steeply pitched roof in all kinds of irregular shapes and a beautiful front-facing gable. The house was painted a dark green with blue and yellow accents. She knew for a fact that Verna would say it was gaudy, but Gen loved it. Big baskets of flowers covered the front, and on the porch, she could see her favorite chair.

"Thank God," she muttered as she parked in the spot that was reserved for her, according to the email she'd received. Closing the top and then turning off the car, she got out hastily before grabbing her bag and heading toward the front of the house. She could hear the noises from the distillery, and then just as she reached the porch, the church bells sounded. A chill ran down her spine as she pushed the door open and headed inside. The inside was like stepping back to the 1920s. The furniture was so regal and irreplaceable. It was stunning, and when a familiar face appeared, coming out the back door of the kitchen, Gen's grin grew.

"I know you!"

Gen laughed. "You sure do. How are you, Delaney?"

Delaney Abbott, a gorgeous brunette with thick lashes and even thicker lips, grinned back at her. "I'm doing great," she gushed before hugging her tight. "I knew that was you when I got the reservation in. You used your real name."

"I did." Gen pulled back, patting her shoulders. "You're working here now?"

"Yeah, just in the morning," she said, waving her off. "With Ms. Neil passing and the new owner getting up to speed, things have been a bit crazy."

Gen's stomach dropped. "No. Huh? What? When?" she stammered in shock.

Delaney's eyes widened. "You didn't know?" she asked slowly, shaking her head while Gen braced her hand to the desk. Memories flooded Gen's mind as she watched Delaney take a deep breath. "Yeah, it was quick, a heart attack."

Tears rushed to her eyes. "I hadn't known. When?"

"It's been about four years now, right after the last time you were here."

"What? Really?"

"Yeah, I sent you a notice for her funeral. I was bummed you didn't show."

"I never got it."

"Well, that's too bad. It was a town affair, you know how we do around here."

Gen nodded as she drew in a breath. She hadn't been expecting that, but then, it was stupid of her to assume everything would be the same. "So are you running the place now?"

Delaney waved her off once more. "Oh no, girl. I only work here when I'm needed. You know I have like eight jobs."

Gen laughed. Delaney was insane. The girl didn't have to work like she did, but ever since Gen had met her, she'd kept so many jobs. Delaney hated being bored and sitting like her mawmaw. So she worked, and she loved it. "You're crazy."

"No, me?" she joked, and they shared a laugh.

"How's your mawmaw?"

"Good, crazy."

Gen smiled. That was good to hear. "Your sister?"

"Great, doing big things up in New York. You hear she's gonna be on *True Love Seekers?*"

Gen scoffed. "No."

"Yes," Delaney said, rolling her eyes at the popular reality show for people who were looking for "the one." "Pathetic."

"But funny."

Delaney laughed before grabbing a key and holding it out to Gen. "This is true. So here you go, the Zoe Jayne suite."

Her brows shot up. "What?"

Delaney just grinned. "Oh yeah, we have a suite just for you."

"When did that happen?" While she was completely taken aback by the sentiment, it did please her to no end. Made her feel all kinds of special.

"A couple years back. The new owner found the books you had dedicated to Ms. Neil and decided that the room you always requested would be yours. Did you not get the announcement about your room?"

Gen shook her head. "What? No?"

"Your mail sucks."

"It does," she decided, taking the key. "But holy crap, that's so nice," she gushed, leaning on the desk as she rubbed her thumb along the key. "Who's the owner? Do I know them?"

Delaney just shrugged, not making eye contact for the first time since Gen had known her. "I think so, but they don't want me to tell you."

Her brows pulled together. "Not tell me? Why on earth?"

"Yeah, I don't know, girl," she said, rolling her eyes. "S-she's weird."

"She?"

"Yeah."

"Hmm." Gen thought that over. "I have no clue."

"Yeah," Delaney laughed. "But yeah, why don't you go get

settled? The porch is open for you, and just let me know when you want dinner."

They hugged once more, and then Gen smiled. "Thanks, Delaney."

"Of course, and by the way, you owe me a drink."

Gen laughed, nodding her head. "I feel you owe me."

"Probably. But we need to go out while you're here, to catch up too."

"Do we still have to go outside of town?"

Delaney grinned. "You know it. We're still drier than a nun's cooch around these parts."

Gen exhaled as she kept in her laughter. "Depressing."

"It is. We make whiskey but can't even drink it here."

Both women laughed before Gen waved, heading up to her room with a grin on her face. Man, she loved this town. Her heart ached for Ms. Neil, and she wished she had known. But then she remembered there was a room just for her. That was insane and amazing. She just wished Ms. Neil were here to share it with her.

Once she got to the room, she unlocked the door and pushed it open as her grin grew. The room, which used to be called the Hummingbird and was a soft pink, was now a bright yellow with dark furniture. Yellow was Gen's favorite color. A painting of the lake was on the wall, along with a big framed print of the cover of her first book. Breathless, she walked in, shutting the door behind her as she took in the room, the classiness of it. It blew her away.

But when she noticed a table that held all her books, she covered her mouth.

"Wow," she breathed as she took out her phone and took a picture. Without thinking, she sent it to her mom and then to Montgomery. Her mom wrote back automatically.

Mom: Oh, Genny. That is amazing! I'll need to go stay!

Before she could write her mother back though, Montgomery wrote back.

Montgomery: So they have a room with your books, and because of that, they're naming it after you?

Rolling her eyes, she tucked her phone into her back pocket.
She wouldn't let him ruin this.

No.

Because this room, the people here, this place, were the start to a trip she needed more than she ever could have realized.

CHAPTER 5

The air was crisp and fresh as Gen stood in the middle of what Spring Grove called their town square. In the middle of the square was the fountain showcasing small children playing in the most epic water battle. It was supposed to be modeled after Old Man McElroy's three boys and his daughter. They were trouble growing up from what she'd heard. Though now, they were all pretty successful but maybe still a bit crazy. She hadn't seen them yet, but she was sure she would. She always did, and boy, were they gorgeous. Which reminded her that she really needed to go on up the hill and check out the distillery. Old Man McElroy would be upset if she didn't check in with him.

But for now, she would explore. With a grin on her lips that was as wide as Kentucky Lake, Gen took in the splendor that was Spring Grove. Around the town square were all the brick buildings that made up downtown. It was almost like an old Western town, all the buildings side by side. The post office, court, and jail all sat together. Though Gen was sure no one had been in that jail in years. As she walked by, she looked ahead at where the stores began. Big windows gave a peek inside, but usually, they were full of whatever the store was selling. Big beautiful flowerpots were everywhere, and in the trees were lights that she knew shone brightly at night. It was all so beautiful, and nothing had changed.

Just like she'd hoped it hadn't.

"Well, holy crap, is that the town celebrity?"

Gen turned and almost came out of her skin when Delaney's mawmaw grinned back at her. Pearl Abbot held her arms open, and Gen went into them, hugging the short, round lady hard as her eyes fell shut. Within seconds, Gen realized she had missed Pearl more than she should have. But how could she not? As they parted, Gen drank in her honorary mawmaw. She had aged in the years that had passed, but her blue eyes were blazing. Her puffy white hair was in a high bun that was probably held together with loads of Aqua Net. She had bright red lips and an even brighter red jumpsuit.

"Mawmaw," she gushed as Pearl held her face in her hands.

"I swear, you're even prettier than the last time I saw you. How long has that been? Five years?"

"Around that," Gen said, covering the older woman's hands with her own. "How are you?"

"Alive, kicking, driving my grandbabies crazy."

"They wouldn't want it any other way."

"Tell that to Delaney. I'm sure she's about to kill me."

"Never," Gen said, waving her off as they parted.

"I have a bone to pick with you, though. Why weren't you at Ms. Neil's funeral?"

"I never knew!" Gen exclaimed, her stomach dropping once more. She still wasn't handling the shock of Ms. Neil's death well. She hated that she had missed the service, but most of all, she hated that she had never gotten the announcement. She wasn't sure why, but maybe they had gotten the wrong address. It hurt, though. She would have wanted to be there. "It kills me, honestly."

"Oh, I know. We figured the news never got to you, and no one had your number. You changed it. You couldn't tell anyone?"

She let her head fall back, shaking her head. "Things have been nuts. I moved in with my fiancé, and then I moved to his phone plan, got a new phone, and yeah, I didn't even think of that. I suck, I'm sorry."

"You do, but I forgive you," she announced with a nod of her head. "Fiancé, huh?"

Gen groaned. "I think we might be separated."

Pearl's bushy white brows pulled together. "What's that mean? I'm old, help me."

Gen giggled, shaking her head. "Problems in paradise, or better yet, DC."

"Oh. That's why you're here, then?"

Gen shrugged. "Actually, no. I wanted to finish my latest novel, but then it evolved into more."

"Oh, well, this is the place to do it. Your second home. Figure you out, girl."

"Yeah," Gen agreed before Pearl took her hand in hers.

"Is he beating you?"

Gen gawked at her, then started laughing. "Not at all."

"Oh, I didn't think so. But I tell you what, these so-called men, I swear. Delaney was with one. He raised his hand once on her, and she smashed his face in with a bat. It was nasty, I tell you."

"Jesus."

"Exactly. She wasn't very close to the cross that morning."

"Can you blame her?"

"No, not at all," Pearl said with a smile. "But this boy, you love him?"

Gen swallowed hard. "I do, but I don't know if I'm in love anymore."

Pearl shook her head before she reached up, cupping Gen's face. "You're a smart girl, Genevieve. It'll all come together."

"I hope so."

"It will. God's working every day."

"He is," Gen agreed as Pearl patted her face.

"That's right. Now I gotta go and help with the planning for the parade. You'll be here for the Fourth?"

Gen shrugged. "I'm unsure how long I'll be staying."

Pearl rolled her eyes. "You'll be here, I feel it."

With that and a sweet wave, Pearl headed in the other direction as Gen just grinned at her retreating back. She loved that lady. So much. Her heart full, even with her issues with Montgomery rearing their ugly head in her brain, she turned, heading toward the south side of the small town.

When she got to Becky's Country Kitchen, Gen heard her stomach rumble, and she knew where she'd be eating lunch. She had spent a lot of time in Becky's. The diner was older than the town, or at least, that was the rumor. She wasn't sure, but they had the best burgers with fried egg she had ever eaten in her life. Along with some damn good fries.

Heading toward it, she waved and smiled at the residents of Spring Grove, feeling every bit at home before pushing open the door to the diner, which wasn't as busy as she expected. Glancing down to her watch, she realized it also wasn't as early as she'd thought. Time flashed by when she was exploring, and that was fine. Fewer people, the faster she could eat. Going straight to the counter, she sat down, grabbing a menu as someone tapped her shoulder.

Before she could turn to see who it was, she heard, "I'll be with ya in a second, love."

She'd know that voice anywhere. She looked toward where Rita Lloyd was rounding the counter with her arms full of plates. She was slower and looked older than Gen had remembered, but there was something about Rita that, even in her later years, would always be beautiful. She had luscious, long brown hair and the brightest blue eyes Gen had ever seen. Well, except those of her son. Her lips were thick and plump, along with a body that was downright banging for a fifty-year-old lady. If Rita looked like that now, trim waist and wide hips, no telling what she had looked like in her prime.

Which was probably how Montgomery's father had gotten involved with her.

Throwing the dishes in the bucket, Rita turned, reaching for her pen and pad from her apron before looking up. When she did, her eyes widened before she squealed.

"Genevieve!"

Rita reached over the counter, and they embraced in a tight hug that took Gen's breath away. "Rita."

"My Lord! You surprised the hell out of me!"

Gen giggled as they parted. "I was hoping to. Though, I wasn't sure you were still working here."

"Girl, I'll die in this diner. How are you? My Lord, you're gorgeous!"

"You're too sweet. I was thinking the same about you."

"Please, I have more gray than I do brown, but I refuse to dye it. My hunny says it gives me a foxy look."

Gen grinned. "A hunny, huh?"

"Oh yes, Roger, my love. He's a good man."

"Good, you deserve it."

"You got that right," she said with a wink. "Let's get some food in you, yeah? The regular?"

"Yes, please."

She grinned back at Gen before she put the order in, ringing the bell. "We missed you at the funeral for Ms. Neil."

"I know," Gen said sadly. "I never got the notice, and I forgot to give my new number to Delaney."

"That's too bad."

"It is. I'm very upset I missed it."

"Well, I'm sure you'll go to her plot, lay some flowers. She'd understand. You're our ritzy celebrity."

Gen just laughed. "Please."

"So how's it going? Life?"

"Good, I'm busy."

"Which is a blessing, ya know."

"It is."

Rita just shot her a grin. "So what brings ya back? I haven't seen ya in, what, four years, right? Tell me, a book need finishing?" she asked, wiping the counter.

"Yup, and I needed to clear my head."

Rita's brows rose at that before she threw the rag in the sink. She then reached for a glass and poured some sweet tea. "Oh? What's going on?"

Rita set it down in front of Gen, and she reached for it as she shrugged. "Boy problems."

"Everyone has those," Rita joked, and Gen laughed along with her. "Is it fixable?"

"I don't know," she answered honestly. She hated that. She didn't want that. She wanted to know for sure what was going on with Montgomery. She wanted him to call her, tell her he missed her, that he loved her, but it had been silence since she left. Except for his dismissive text about her books, she hadn't heard from him. It was depressing.

"Well, it'll work out. You always said this town was magic for you."

"Yeah, it is."

Rita gave her another wink as she moved around, refilling the ketchup. "How's your momma?"

"She's good."

"Your daddy?"

"Fine."

"Good, since I haven't seen them, I'm guessing you're staying out of trouble?"

Gen just grinned. "So far."

"Let's keep it that way."

Gen took a long swig of her tea and asked, "How is everything here? Still the same?"

"Always," Rita answered with a wide smile. "The way we love it."

"You and Roger living in the same house?"

"Yup," she said with a grin. "He wants to do all kinds of stuff, but we're so lazy."

Gen laughed, but she had to force it. She wanted so badly to ask about Rita's son, but she knew she had no right to. She hadn't seen or heard from Theo in eons. She shouldn't even want to know anything about him. She had a fiancé. She was supposed to be happy.

Supposed to be.

"You like your room at the Blu?"

Gen nodded, her face lighting up. "I do. I love it so much."

"I do too. A lot."

Nodding once more, Gen said, "I heard there are new owners of the Blu. I haven't met them yet."

And just like Delaney, Rita froze. Looking over at Gen, Rita swallowed hard. "Yeah."

"I haven't even seen them. Isn't that insane?"

"Yeah."

Gen shot her a look, but before she could ask more, the ring of the bell sounded that her food was ready. Reaching for it, Rita laid it in front of Gen.

"Now eat up, my love. I've got some work to do. You're a distraction for sure!"

With that, she walked away, and Gen realized she was really starting to get annoyed.

Why wouldn't anyone tell her who the damn owner of the Blu was?

CHAPTER 6

Complete and utter peace enveloped Gen as she stepped onto the back porch of the Blu. It was purely majestic. The lake was rushing up on the man-made shore and all along the dock that Gen could still remember being built. It was when she first came there, and it only took the crew of misfits Ms. Neil had hired three days. Theo was a part of the crew, and his pay went to Gen's lodging at the Blu since his mom wouldn't let him have a girl in his bed in her house. They weren't underage, but she still stuck to her guns. A grin pulled at Gen's lips as her fingers danced along her laptop, her eyes gazing out across the backyard.

She'd wanted so desperately for nothing to change, but it had. Ms. Neil wasn't there, and neither were the canoes along the bank or the beach chairs. It was much cleaner, classier almost, like a real business was being run. Not that Ms. Neil hadn't run a true business, but with her, it was more a home she had people to stay in. Now, it was obvious this place was being run for a profit, and Gen wasn't sure how that made her feel.

Especially since she hadn't met the new owners.

It had been five days since she had arrived. She had written six chapters in that time, and at that rate, she was going to be done in no time. She wasn't sure if that excited her or upset her. She knew the point of coming here was to write, but when she was done, would she be expected to go home? Because she didn't want to. Not yet, at least. She was just getting comfortable. She was still busy seeing everyone, and she wasn't nearly done exploring. She knew that made her a horrible person, and she knew she really needed to think what that meant. She just didn't want to deal with it. Not when the sun was kissing her face and the stillness was exciting her.

Being there, she couldn't help but wonder if maybe she wasn't cut out for city life.

Another thing she needed to assess.

Rolling her eyes at her endless list of things to examine in her life, she sat down in her spot and opened her laptop to where her chapter and characters were waiting. She felt giddy not needing her headphones as she jumped in, her fingers flying over the keys.

"Angel, I can't."

"You can," she demanded, looking over her shoulder at him, spreading her ass apart for him. Her body was burning with heat, flushed. And fucking hell, he wanted her. He wanted to push his cock so deep inside of her ass, he wouldn't be able to think, but he couldn't.

He wouldn't.

"Angel," he tried to say, his voice cracking as he watched her squeeze her ass cheeks, her eyes searing into his. His nickname for her, angel, wasn't something he said often, but when it came to her, he found no other word to describe her.

She took him straight to heaven. With just a look.

His beautiful angel.

"I could hurt you. You're so small, and you've never done it—"

"First time for everything," she said over him, and his hands shook as he met her gaze. "I want you to fuck me, Travis. I want you inside of me. Now."

His heart skipped a beat. How did this happen? She was his best friend's sister. Baby sister. He knew better, but fucking hell, he was about to fuck her hard.

Because she was his.

When her phone rang, Gen glanced over at it, her breath catching. She wanted so much for it to be Montgomery, but it was her mother. Only a little disappointed, since she hadn't spoken to her mother since she had arrived, she picked it up. "Hey Mom."

"Hey, honey, how are you? How's it going?"

"Great, words are pouring out of me."

"Wonderful. Is everything still utterly beautiful there? I was always so jealous of that place. It reminds me so much of back home in Georgia."

Exhaling deeply, Gen leaned back in her chair, and it gave a bit so the sun kissed her cheeks even more. It was such a peaceful day. She could hear the sounds of the distillery on the hill, and she figured she'd need to make a trip up there.

"It is. I love it here. You should come visit before I leave."

"Maybe, we'll have to see."

"Yeah," she said, her voice trailing off because if she had her way, she'd never leave. "I really don't want to leave, Mom."

Fawn paused for a moment before she cleared her throat. "Well, we both know that Montgomery isn't going to move there, Genevieve."

Gen shrugged, closing her eyes. "I know."

"Then that probably won't happen."

"I'm just saying. I don't want to."

She paused once more. "Genevieve."

"What?"

"What's going on?"

She cleared her throat. "We haven't spoken since I left. Well, no, I take that back. I texted him about my room, and he was a smartass about it."

"Why? Because you went?"

"That and because he wants me to quit writing."

Her mother took in a quick breath. "What? It's your job."

"He wants me to be a housewife, he says. I guess I should have figured that out since he never really implied that he wanted me to get another career. I want more from my life than that. I want to be successful but also a great mom, ya know?"

"Oh."

Gen's brows pulled together. "Oh?"

"I feel that was a bit of a dig at me."

"Not at all. You only wanted a mom life, and I want both."

"Well, I mean, you won't have time for writing when the kids come anyway," her mother treaded gently, and Gen scoffed.

"I'll make time. I'll write with a kid on the tit, I'm good."

"I don't doubt that," she said softly. "But I don't think Mont understands that."

"He doesn't. He wants me to be his mom, or hell, you, and I don't want that. I don't know, Mom," she said, frustrated. "Maybe I should call off the wedding."

Her mother gasped before she started rambling. "Oh no, Gen, that's a little dramatic. I'm sure this can be fixed."

"Maybe, but I don't want to get trapped in a marriage where my husband doesn't support what I do."

Fawn didn't answer for a long time before she said, "I understand, but, Gen, if you call this wedding off, you're saying goodbye to him permanently because he won't stand for that. Or really, his momma won't. And since he's basically still hanging on to that umbilical cord, that might not go well."

Gen snorted as she nodded. She knew her mom didn't mean to be funny, but it was since it was the truth. Montgomery was the biggest momma's boy Gen had ever met. It hadn't ever bothered her before, but now, with the wedding and everything else... Yeah, it was a real problem.

"Oh, Genny, what am I going to do with you?"

Gen smiled. "What does that mean?"

"I just want to know you're taken care of, and I feel like you're running."

"Mom, I'll always be taken care of. I don't need anyone to do it for me."

"I mean by a man, and Mont would take good care of you."

"Yeah, but he wouldn't support me even a bit."

"That's unfortunate. I have dinner with Verna tonight. I'll bring it up."

"Ew, please don't."

"Okay." Gen knew she would anyway, so she let it go. "All right, well, you finish that book and then really do some soul-searching, okay? Can you honestly live without Mont? Don't you love him?"

When Gen couldn't answer automatically, she felt her stomach drop.

Did she love him?

"I don't know," she answered, more to herself than her mother. "He really hurt me the other day. He accused me of coming here to cheat on him."

"What in the hell? Is he insane?"

"He must be."

"Who in the world would you... Oh Lord, is that drug lord still there?"

Gen snorted as she shook her head. "He wasn't a drug lord. More of a mover of the drugs, and hell if I know. I haven't seen him."

"Goodness me. I'd forgotten all about that guy."

Gen hadn't. "Yeah."

"Okay, well, don't get into any trouble. And if you see that guy, run. Please. Like you should have when he cornered you in the clubhouse."

"I think I cornered him."

"Genevieve, don't ruin my beautiful image of you as a sweet and innocent teenager."

That had her guffawing. "Mom, come on. I went home with Montgomery after our first date. I'm no Sister Mary. I write smut, as Montgomery constantly reminds me, for goodness' sake."

"Lord. Please stop. I don't know what you do. I'm hanging up."

"Love you."

"Love you more."

With a grin still in place, Gen went to hang up, but then her mother said, "And please, really think this through, my love. Don't let Montgomery go without considering all of the repercussions."

Her smile dropped then as she swallowed. "I hear ya, Mom."

She hung up and leaned back. It was all just so complicated. Why couldn't he be supportive? Why couldn't he just understand that she wouldn't stop writing? Since her phone was still in her hand, she texted him.

Genevieve: Why haven't I heard from you?

When he didn't answer right away, she told herself he was working, but she knew damn well he had his phone on him. He always did.

Before she could go back to work, she heard, "Hey, Gen, you hungry?"

Gen looked over her shoulder at Delaney who was standing in the door to the kitchen on the other side of the porch. Tilting her head in curiosity, Gen said, "Hey, what are you doing here? I thought the new girl was starting?"

"She's a no-show, like everyone else in this town, and since I owe—" She stopped, her lips pressing together as her nose wrinkled up. "I'm here. You hungry?"

Gen's eyes narrowed. "You owe whom?"

"No one. Food. You. Is it happening?"

Gen laughed. "Yes. Please. Thanks," she called as the door shut. A grin sat on her face. She wasn't sure what the deal was with the mystery of the Blu's owner, but she was surprised how much she didn't care. It was probably some girl she didn't even know. Maybe a fan who was nervous around her or something, because everyone in Spring Grove loved Gen. She was awesome, how could they not? She chuckled to herself.

When the door opened once more, she looked back as Delaney started toward her, a plate in hand. When she set it down, Gen's eyes widened. "Oh, shut up."

"Oh, yes. The Blu's famous fried pickles."

"Holy mother of God," Gen groaned as she took a bite of the fried goodness and moaned. They were perfectly cooked and downright scrumptious. The last time she'd had this fried magic was when Theo... Her brows immediately drew in as she glanced up to Delaney. "These are wonderful," she said slowly. "You make them?"

Delaney laughed. "No, girl. I can cook, but I can't cook that. The chef did."

"Is the chef the owner?"

"Maybe," she drawled. "But word on the street is this is your favorite, and since you're our only guest, here you go."

Gen paused her eating. "Why am I the only guest?"

"I don't know," Delaney said simply, shrugging her shoulders. But it was a lie. "Slow month?"

"It's peak tourist time. Everyone is in town."

"Yeah, I don't know," she said while looking everywhere but at Gen. Which meant one thing.

More lies.

With a grin, Gen leaned on her hand. "Hey, Del, you remember Theo Hudson? I saw his momma the other day."

"Oh, yeah. She's a hoot." Delaney struggled for words, and Gen could tell she wanted to get away.

But she wasn't going anywhere until Gen had some answers. "What about Theo?"

Delaney blinked. "Yeah, I don't know."

"You don't?"

"Nope."

Oh, she was lying through her teeth. "Really? Don't you talk to his mom?"

"I do."

"And she doesn't talk about Theo?"

Delaney started to get flustered. "Yeah, I mean, I don't know. I gotta go."

"No, you don't," Gen said laughing. "I was just curious."

She shrugged. "Well, y'all were too hot for words, so I expect you would be."

A grin pulled at Gen's lips. The five years she'd had with Montgomery couldn't even come close to those two weeks of passion with Theo. Wow. That was pathetic. When her phone dinged, she looked down to see it was a text from Montgomery.

Montgomery: Have nothing to say.

Her face turned hot with annoyance, and before she could even think it through, she asked, "Say, what are you doing tonight?"

Delaney looked back at her, her eyes boring into Gen. "I think I might be going to the bar with you. For that drink you owe me."

A sinful grin came over Gen's lips. All her thoughts of Montgomery, her mom, and her life outside of Spring Grove were gone, and Gen had one thing on her mind.

Finding out what in the world was going on with Theo Hudson.

Her fiancé's half brother.

She knew it was wrong. She knew she should take her mom's advice and not worry about it, but something was up.

And she needed to know.

So with a nod and a sneaky grin, Gen said, "I think you might be right."

CHAPTER 7

The Drunken Barrel sat right on the county line and was something out of an old Western. It reminded her of a saloon, and she wasn't even the least bit surprised to see the same old men taking up residence on their barstools. She couldn't remember their names, probably since they had never talked to her, but she'd never forget their leathered faces or their bushy eyebrows. The whole room smelled of whiskey and cigarettes, but it didn't bother Gen. It excited her.

"It hasn't changed a bit."

Delaney rolled her eyes. "Does anything in this town?" Gen smiled over at her as they went to the bar, sitting down before Delaney concluded, "Obviously I love it, since I haven't left."

"Exactly. This is your town," Gen agreed, and Delaney grinned. "You work everywhere."

Delaney laughed. "I do. I love money."

"Do you even have time to spend it?"

Delaney nodded. "Yup, like now." Holding up her hand up, Delaney called, "Two shots of whiskey and two beers."

The bartender nodded, and Gen then glanced to Delaney. "I'm supposed to be buying."

"Oh, I know. But this first one is on me, to welcome you and all."

Gen grinned as she nodded, looking her friend over. She was wearing a body-hugging dress, her long brown hair down along her shoulders. Her makeup was dark and her lips bright red. Gen suspected she wanted to show off a bit. "So, are you dating anyone?"

A sweet smile pulled at Delaney's lips as she nodded. "Larry from the body shop."

Gen paused and then made a face. "The guy with no teeth?"

Delaney laughed. "He's missing one."

"It's a front one, though?"

"Well, yeah, but it's fine. He's still handsome, and he treats me like a lady."

"That's all that matters," Gen said, and Delaney nodded in agreement.

"It is, and since I've been through everyone else, this is my last chance in Spring Grove. I'm going to have to go back on a dating site next."

"FarmersOnly.com?"

"I hate you."

"Plenty of fish is good too, apparently."

"Really, stop."

Gen laughed as she shook her head. "Being in a relationship isn't all that great."

As their drinks were placed on the bar, Delaney clucked her tongue. "Oh no, trouble in paradise? You're with that rich guy, right?"

Gen rolled her eyes. "That narrows it down."

"Well, you do come from a fancy-dancy place."

"Well, I'm not fancy-dancy."

"No, but that's your roots." Delaney took her shot and let out a harsh sigh. "And you know who I mean. Theo's half brother. What's his name, Marshall? Mitch? Miguel?"

"Montgomery." After taking her shot, Gen made a face. "Miguel?"

"What? It seemed right," Delaney laughed before she took a long pull of her beer. "Are y'all married?"

"No, not yet. Three weeks."

"Oh."

"Yeah," she said slowly, clearing her throat. "I'm not sure I want to do it anymore."

"Why?"

"I don't know, he's being a dick and he doesn't support my career."

"Hasn't he always been a dick?"

Gen gave her a dry look. "He's a good man, he just doesn't want me to have a career. He wants me to be a stay-at-home mom or some shit. That's not me."

"Why are you just now finding out about him not supporting you?"

Gen's stomach hurt as she took a pull of her beer to replace the sourness in her gut. "'Cause I'm an idiot? I was comfortable. Sex was good, things were easy. And now, it's not."

"I feel that was something to fix a while back, or at least, to discuss."

"I guess we ignored it. Like I said, the sex used to be good. Now we're both just distracted."

"No one is too distracted for sex."

Gen shrugged. "They can be." When Delaney sent her a dubious look, Gen shrugged again. "We are, at least."

"Maybe 'cause y'all shouldn't be together. Or maybe y'all fell out of love?"

Gen sighed as she tapped the bar with her empty shot glass, wanting another one. "I don't know."

"Well then, don't do it."

"I haven't even really spoken to him since I left. It's been a crappy text here and there. Isn't that pathetic?"

"It is," Delaney agreed, shaking her head. "What's his deal?"

"He didn't want me to come."

"Why?"

Gen shrugged. "Who knows. He brought up me cheating on him, when I'd never. He was the one to cheat on me."

Delaney held her hands up, her eyes wide. "Whoa, he cheated on you?"

"Yeah, like three years ago. We went to counseling."

Delaney cleared her throat, not looking the least bit convinced. "My mawmaw always says, once a cheater, always a cheater."

Gen shrugged as her shot glass was filled, and she knocked it back quickly. "Yeah, I don't know."

Delaney's eyes widened as she looked away, nodding her head. "Well, putting the cheating aside, do you think he can change his mind on your career?"

Gen shook her head. "No, and I think I always knew that."

"Then I vote to leave him."

Gen laughed. "It's harder than that, I think—"

"No, it's not," Delaney interjected. "If you're not happy, you'll never be happy. Things don't get better because you want them to. There has to be some bend in a relationship. It takes two, and if he isn't wanting to bend now, he'll never bend." Gen just blinked, Delaney's words hitting her straight in the heart. "Mark my words, Genevieve. If you don't call it off now, you'll be stuck, and you'll be very unhappy for the rest of your days. I'd rather live here, where I'm basically looking under rocks for someone to love me, rather than be in a relationship where I'm not valued."

A little breathless, Gen shifted her gaze, taking a pull of her beer. Looking back at her longtime friend—even though they hadn't stayed in contact unless she was in Spring Grove—she smiled. "When did you get so smart?"

"2015, I think, when I got dumped for having a fat ass and not having any intentions of changing that."

Gen shook her head. "His loss."

"Exactly. I'd already lost over a hundred pounds by then. I'm done."

Gen smiled, remembering when Delaney was larger, but her friend had always been beautiful. It was her heart; Delaney would do anything for anyone. Just like her mawmaw would. They were good people, that was for sure. "I think you're perfect."

"Sound like my mawmaw," she laughed, and Gen smiled. "I'm good, and I know that. And you should know that too. You deserve someone who will be there beside you no matter what. No matter if you want to have ten kids or none. If you want to write or if you want to eat Ho Hos and watch TV. It doesn't matter because they love you, ya know?"

Gen nodded. She felt exactly the same, but why couldn't Montgomery? "Yeah, I know."

"So don't be dumb."

Laughing, she leaned into Delaney, shaking her head. "Don't hold back there, friend."

"Never," she said with a wink before she held up her beer, which Gen clinked hers to. "You're too pretty and nice not to be loved for who you are."

"Thanks, Delaney."

"Anytime."

The ladies shared a long look, a look that told Gen she was better than this and she knew it. But could she throw it all away? Five years was a long time to be with someone, to love them, or to think you loved them. Jesus, had she really been wasting that much of her life? Before she could really commit to that idea, the jukebox changed, and Keith Urban's "The Fighter" started blaring through the bar. Hopping up, Delaney took her hand and then dragged her out to the dance floor where they both let the music take control, the whiskey allowing them both to let go and dance like no one was watching. Though Gen knew everyone was since they were the only ones on the floor.

They danced and sang for what seemed like hours, getting more beer and even more shots. They were having a blast. When they both sat down, ordering another round, Gen leaned into the bar, inhaling hard as she reached for her phone out of her purse. She had four missed calls from Montgomery.

Shit.

"Oh! There's Larry!"

Before Gen could comment, Delaney hopped up and was heading toward where Larry Yarbrough was walking in with some guys behind him. Gen didn't get a good look at anyone though because she looked back at her phone, seeing that Montgomery had texted her too.

Montgomery: And see, when I have something to say, you don't have time to answer me.

Rolling her eyes, she got up and headed out the side door into the hot summer night. Hitting Montgomery's number, she waited as the phone rang.

"I called and texted."

"I know, that's why I'm calling you back," she answered, annoyed. "I didn't hear it before."

"Are you drunk?"

She closed her eyes, pressing her lips together. "Tipsy at best."

"So you're out drinking? I thought you were working."

"I worked all day. I'm having some fun with Delaney Abbot. You remember her, don't you?"

"The fat chick?"

"Montgomery, that's rude."

"What? It's true."

"No, it's not," Gen defended, shaking her head. "Yes, she is thicker."

"So you're out drinking with her? Only her? 'Cause I hear music."

"I'm at a bar."

He scoffed and then bit out dismissively, "Okay, well go have fun."

"Wait," she said, praying he didn't hang up. "I'm just letting loose."

"You had to leave to do that?"

"No, not at all. I've come to write, and that's what I've been doing. I don't want to fight."

"Well, I don't want my fiancée parading all over God's green earth, getting drunk and whatnot when she told me she was getting away to work. It's bullshit. If you don't want to be with me, don't."

"Mont, I'm working, I am. I just wanted to come out with my friend for a night."

"Yeah, I'm sure. Go have fun, maybe I'll do the same. Go get shit-faced and fuck around."

"I'm not doing that! What the hell?"

"I bet. If that weren't the case, then you could have 'worked' here."

"I need my special place. I was struggling at home. I was stressed out."

"Stressed out from picking out words for a book? It must be hard choosing between cock and dick. You poor thing, try being me. I am stressed, I am busy making money for our family, and you're just playing around. Get it together, Genevieve."

She was speechless. How dare he. "Wow, do you really think that's all I do?"

"I don't fucking care, but I do care when you're out, getting drunk, and probably looking for someone to fuck."

"I don't understand, Mont. Why are you acting like this? I've never cheated!"

"Nope, but you went to the place where he lives in, the one you lost. Remember when you told me that?" She rolled her eyes. It had been so long ago when Gen had apparently admitted to missing Theo and wishing he hadn't gotten away. Eons ago. What was Montgomery's problem?

"Oh my God, I was drunk, and I still don't believe I actually said that!"

"You did. I was there. So go on, find him. Fuck him. I don't fucking care."

"That's not my intention at all. I'm here to work—"

But before she could finish, the line went dead, and she let her hand fall to her hip. "Asshole."

Tears stung her eyes as she shook her head. What the hell was happening? She had just wanted to go out drinking. That was it. Let loose, have fun with her girlfriend. Why was he treating her like this? Was she in the wrong?

"Wow, he sounds like a dick." Looking in the direction of where the voice came from, she could see a guy push off the wall of the bar. She hadn't even realized he was there. As he snuffed out his cigarette, he walked by her, and Lord was he big. Tall, long legs in a pair of worn jeans, and a thin shirt. His arms were covered in tattoos, but she couldn't see his face in the shadows. All she could make out was his dark, bushy beard. Before she could answer him, or even comment, really, he reached for the door, pulling it open, and heading inside without another word.

Exhaling heavily, Gen murmured, "Yeah." She really didn't understand how this had all happened. She had no ill intentions. She wanted to write, she wanted to hang with her friend, and spend time in her town. What was wrong with that?

Nothing.

Nothing was wrong with that.

Fuck him. If Montgomery wanted to act like that, well, fuck him!

Stuffing her phone into her back pocket, she pulled the door open with all the force she had in her. It slammed against the wall as she walked straight up to the bar where she'd left her purse— something you could only do in a town the size of Spring Grove. Leaning on the bar, she tapped her shot glass to the bar and yelled out, "Six more, please!"

The bartender just smiled, shaking his head as Delaney looked down the bar at her. She was leaning on Larry, a grin on her face, until suddenly, it was gone. Her eyes widened, and her mouth parted, confusing Gen, but then she realized Delaney wasn't looking at her. She was looking at the guy two stools down from Gen.

Unsure why Delaney was focused on a stranger, Gen hollered out, "You gonna come help me with these?"

Delaney's mouth moved as the bartender went to work filling the glasses, but no words were leaving her mouth. Gen went to say more, but then the guy beside her was moving. "Put those on my tab."

Gen waved him off. "Thank you, but they're for my girlfriend and me."

"She's busy. Do them with me," he suggested, reaching for one and handing it to her. She took it, a little taken aback, but then she looked up into his face. His eyes were blazing blue, crinkled at the sides. She swore she knew those eyes. Holding up the glass, he murmured, "To old times."

Her stomach dropped, her eyes widening as the realization of who was standing in front of her dawned on her. Before she could move, talk, or even take the shot, the bartender said, "Theo, you don't have a tab."

A grin pulled at his lips and basically knocked Gen unconscious, just like it had when they were younger. "Start me one."

He clinked his glass to hers before downing the shot. Letting out a loud grunt, he slammed it on the bar, his eyes still trained on hers. Gen wasn't even sure she was breathing. "You gonna shoot that?"

Her mouth was dry as she stared at him in disbelief. "Theo?"

CHAPTER 8

"**O**ne and only."

Gen felt like she was going to drop the shot as he clinked the next one to hers and shot it with ease. Her heart was slamming against her chest, and her throat was closing up as she drank him in. His dark locks were disheveled and curled defiantly against his ear. His jaw was thick and full of even more unruly curly hair. But his eyes were still the exact same, blazing blue with dark lashes that were long and straight. He wasn't skinny like he used to be, instead thick with muscle, and boy was he toned. Gone was the boy she had known, leaving behind a man who was meant to be admired.

Or worshiped.

"Well, hot damn, Genny, I'm done. You gonna catch up?"

But still, she couldn't move. It was like she was slammed back in time, to the moment she had seen him at the country club. He was the talk of the clubhouse, Bruce Hudson's bastard kid from another woman. He was rowdy and every bit the savage that some whore from a diner would raise. Everyone hated him the moment they heard of him. Everyone except Gen. She was intrigued by the "monster" who had popped up and threatened the Hudsons' marriage. But when she saw him walking into the club in his thin, crisp white tee, frayed, worn jeans, and cowboy boots, she realized he wasn't a monster. He was a gorgeous bad boy she knew her dad would hate. And since teenage Gen was looking for anything to piss her parents off, she was attracted to him within seconds, and she got exactly what she wanted.

Great sex, a good time, and pissed-off parents.

Looking up into his face, she still saw traces of that bad boy, and her insides warmed as she gazed at him. He laughed, shaking his head. "You're looking at me like you're seeing a ghost."

She swallowed hard. "I feel like I am."

He smiled. "Nope, I'm real. Wanna pinch me?"

Bracing her hand on the bar, she shook her head before throwing back one of the shots, then another, before finishing the last one. Letting out a quick hiss, she took a long pull of her beer before giving him a sideways glance to make sure he was still there.

He was.

Looking even more scrumptious than she remembered him.

Oh, this was bad.

"Wow."

He smiled, showing the little chip on his tooth he had gotten on their road trip because of her. She had gone to open the door right as he reached for it, intending to open it for her, but she smacked him in the mouth with the door before he could. She had felt awful, but he just laughed it off. Holy crap, she was standing with Theo Hudson, in a bar.

Just like Montgomery accused her of.

Her heart ached as she turned, leaning into the bar. "I shouldn't be here."

"I'd say you're in the perfect spot," he muttered, and when she chanced a glance, he was looking her up and down. "Mercy, Genny, have you gotten hotter?"

He said it.

Mercy.

Fuck, she was done for.

Swallowing hard, hoping to push her damn heart out of her throat, she glanced over at him. "I'm engaged."

He didn't seem surprised as he said, "I can't tell you you're hot because of that?"

"No."

"Well, I don't know where you heard those rules, but I'm gonna say it if I want. Because when someone is as gorgeous as you are, it's my duty to make sure they know that."

Her eyes fell shut as she gripped the bar, all those feelings, those crazy, unruly ones from back then, slamming back into her gut. Damn it. "I gotta go."

But when she turned, trying to get the hell out of there, her foot got stuck in the rung of the stool, and the next thing she knew, she was flying through the air headed straight for the dirty-ass floor. Lights went off in her head, and she cried out right as she felt something hot rushing from her nose.

"Whoa, Genny, you okay?" She felt his hands on her, and then she was upright, her hand going over her nose as the blood rushed out of it. "Shit, Clive, a towel."

She closed her eyes, trying to keep her sanity because even though her nose was bleeding and everyone gushed over her, helping her, all she could think or feel was him. All of him.

Theo.

Squeezing her eyes shut as the world spun, she felt his hand run along her neck, holding her in place as he placed the rag on her rose. "Damn, you fell hard."

"Shit, is she gonna have a black eye?" she heard Delaney ask, but Gen couldn't answer. She could feel the whiskey tickling the back of her throat, and it was taking everything in her to keep it down.

"Sure looks like it. She hit that floor hard," someone added, and Gen winced. That was all she needed.

"I can't have a black eye when I get married."

"Well, angel, I don't think you have a choice," Theo told her, moving his thumb along her nose. She cringed from the pain, opening her eyes, her gaze meeting his dark one. Her breath caught as his lips quirked at the side. "No matter, though. I'm sure you'll still be as gorgeous as ever. It's kinda crazy, but I swear you haven't changed a bit."

She swallowed hard, pushing the whiskey back. "I'm fatter."

"Nah, not even a bit."

Her eyes filled with tears as he moved his thumb across the bridge of her nose, a grin sitting on his lips. "It isn't broken, which is good." Heat filled her gut, her heart stopping in her chest as his eyes bored into hers. "Man, Genny, it's really good to see you."

"You too," she muttered as he pulled the rag away, checking to see if her nose was still bleeding. It must have been because he put the rag back, giving her a smile.

"Why you running off, then?"

She looked down at his hand. It was large, holding the whole rag with ease, and thick. She also noticed he didn't have a ring on. He wasn't married. Which didn't mean a thing, and she hated the little swirl of hope that started up in her stomach. "I shouldn't be with you."

"Why's that?" he laughed. "Your parents still hate me?"

She sputtered with laughter, and his own laughter grew. "I think they'll always hate you."

"Probably," he decided, pulling the rag away again. When he saw there was no more blood flow, he threw it on the bar. "But I don't care."

When he glanced back at her, her stomach twisted as she got lost in his eyes. "I shouldn't be here."

"Here? Or with me?"

"Both," she answered, completely lost in his eyes. "He's already pissed at me."

"The dude from outside? On the phone? Is that the fiancé?"

Her stomach dropped. "Yeah."

"Well, he's a douche. You're more than welcome to hang out with old friends, have fun. You're on vacation, for God's sake."

Her lips pressed together as her heart beat so hard, it was hurting her ears. "According to him, I should only be working."

"Working, huh? Is that what brought you back? You haven't been here in a while."

"Yeah," she said slowly, pulling her gaze away. She knew she should go. Run, hightail it, but she couldn't move. She...she...she didn't want to. "It's been a while, and I've missed it. But yeah, I'm here finishing a book."

"I've seen how successful you've gotten," he said, a little smile pulling at his lips. "I'm really proud of you, Genny. You said you were gonna do something big one day."

Her face broke into a grin. "I did, huh?"

"Yeah, I remember it like it was yesterday."

She nodded. "Me too." She looked up, and he was watching her. Her body lit on fire as she started to ramble. "What are you doing now? Still running drugs?"

He laughed, shaking his head, smacking the bar in the process. "Nah. That was a one and done kind of deal. Spending two years in jail as a kid will scare you right out of that."

Her jaw dropped. "You actually spent time in jail?"

He laughed. "Yeah. I thought you knew that."

"I mean, I guess I did, but I didn't realize it was that long."

He nodded. "Yeah, apparently it's illegal to run drugs. But good thing for me is I had a daddy who didn't want anyone knowing about it. So they gave me a slap on the wrist."

"Two years is a slap on the wrist?" she gasped.

"It should have been ten."

"Good Lord!"

He turned slightly, his knee brushing hers. She knew she should move, she even told herself to move. But instead, she sat right there. The contact sent heat all throughout her body. When she met his gaze, she could see he felt it too. With a sinister smile and a deep voice that rattled her soul, he said, "Yeah, I was a bad, bad boy."

She was breathless, but somehow got out, "Was?" Shit. Shit. Shit! "Ignore that, that was the alcohol."

He grinned, all his teeth showing like she was the little tweety bird and he was the cat. "Mmm-hmm."

"It was!"

"Sure," he said, but even she knew that wasn't all the alcohol. How could it be? He looked...bad. Like someone she wrote about. The kind of hero who would pick her up by her waist, slam her down on a table, and fuck her from behind while pressing his thumb so hard against her asshole, she'd be screaming his names for hours.

Great. Now she was turned on.

Or maybe it really was the whiskey because she was feeling it for sure. Her fingers were numb, her mind a little fuzzy—yeah, she needed to get out of there. "I really need to go."

"No, don't," he said, stopping her when she tried to get up. "What's the rush? I don't even know your little so-called fiancé's name."

Her stomach clenched as she looked away, shaking her head.

"Yeah, you do."

He laughed, shaking his head. "What? My older half brother?" When she didn't answer, just met his gaze, his laughter faltered, and soon he was staring at her. "No way."

She shrugged. "I've been with him for five years."

"What the fuck? How could you be with him a day?"

"He's a good man."

"He's a fucking asshole, just like his dad."

"Your dad."

"Fuck that. My mom is my dad and my mom. Jesus, I thought —" He paused, shaking his head. "Wow, really, Genny? Why? Why him?"

She looked away. "Because I love him."

"Liar," he yelled, and when she looked up, he was crossing his arms over his wide, thick chest. "You may have loved him at one point, but not anymore."

"What? That's preposterous."

He laughed some more. "I always did like those big ole words you used, but it's true. When you love someone, Genevieve Stone, you love with your whole self. I've seen it, and that's not what I see right now."

Her heart stopped dead in her chest. "You don't know what you're talking about," she stammered, pushing back the whiskey-vomit combo that was burning the back of her throat. "I do love him."

Why was she lying?

But Theo just laughed, shaking his head. "You don't. 'Cause if you did, you wouldn't have let him hang up on you. You would have called back until he listened to you. You're a fighter."

She was flabbergasted. She hadn't seen this man in years, and he was sitting here talking like he still knew her. "You don't even know me."

"Oh, I may not know this version of you, which I'm sure I've made known. You may be even more gorgeous, but, Genny, I know your soul."

Her lips pressed together as she just blinked up at him. But his eyes, man, they were fierce. His words weren't just words; that wasn't Theo. His words were true, from his heart, and that was bad, so very bad. This couldn't be happening. She couldn't be with him. His claim of them just catching up was complete bullshit. There was no catching up with them. There was too much unfinished history between them, and she had to get out of there. But she didn't move because she wanted to know what the hell he was implying. She knew what she was feeling—which was wrong on so many levels—but was he feeling that too? Shit, why did that matter? And why did his eyes still make her skin break out in gooseflesh!

Damn it! This was bad. So damn bad.

Leave. Leave now, Genevieve.

But when she opened her mouth, with every intention of

forming a sentence, she found that, instead, it was to promptly puke all over both of their laps.

She tried to stop, Theo tried to move, but their legs were locked together. And before she knew it, she was puking up the entire contents of her stomach.

The damage was done.

Awesome.

Looking up, embarrassment burning her face and her neck, she met his shocked gaze before she asked, "Can you hand me that rag, please?"

CHAPTER 9

en wiggled her toes.

Then her fingers.

When she didn't feel like she was going to puke, she slowly opened her eyes. But when the sun hit her eyes, she winced, squeezing them shut again as she swallowed back the bile. Reaching for the pillow beside her, she covered her face as she groaned loudly into it. What did she do to herself last night? She knew damn well what she did, but damn it, she was usually good when she drank. But then, had she ever drunk so much not only to forget her...her...well, whatever the fuck Montgomery was? And then, Theo? Nope, and the whiskey in Spring Grove was always stronger.

Whiskey: 1. Gen: 0.

She knew better, she did, but yet, there she was, lying with a pillow on her face. Wishing for death. It was obvious no work would be getting done, especially if she couldn't find a way downstairs to get some food to soak up all the whiskey still swirling in her gut. She gagged at just the thought of trying to shove something down her throat.

I could help shove something down your throat, angel, something thick and long. You ready?

A grin pulled at her lips as Travis spoke in her head. He wanted so badly to be written, and she wanted to write him, but the problem with that was moving. Moving wasn't an option right now. Swallowing tentatively, she exhaled. What in God's name was she thinking last night? All she wanted was info on either Theo or the people who owned the Blu. But what she got was another fight with Montgomery and puking all over Theo. Other stuff happened, but she didn't want to think of those things. She couldn't. Theo was ancient history. He was probably already married, seven kids, and all that jazz. Not that it mattered, but man, she bet his wife was one lucky lady.

Because Gen could still feel his lips on hers. There was something about his lips, the bottom one larger than the top. When he devoured her mouth, his bottom lip would almost suffocate hers, and she lived for it. His kisses, they were...heaven. And like clockwork, every time, he'd pull back and whisper *mercy* against her lips. Two weeks, that's all it had been, but it felt like a lifetime. Seeing him again, those frayed, worn jeans, the tight tee on his shoulders, his lips, his eyes, his beard, it was all so overwhelming, and those feelings she shouldn't be feeling came back tenfold.

It wasn't fair, really. These feelings that were drowning her senses like the whiskey had, how could she feel them? She was supposed to be in love with Montgomery; he was supposed to be her forever. But if that was the case, why was she wanting so badly to find Theo, sit down, and just talk. She wanted to know everything. Where he had been, what he had been doing, who he was with. Anything and everything, but she knew if she allowed herself to do that, it would lead to more. They'd slept together the second night of knowing each other. Yeah, it was mostly because she wanted to piss off her parents, but once she got some, it was all she wanted. Him. All of him.

But Montgomery...

Fuck.

She had to stay away from Theo.

That was the only option.

She had to stick to the plan, stick to her reasons for being there. She had to finish her book, she had to go home, and then she could figure out things with Montgomery. If they were gonna call everything off, then fine, they'd come to that decision together. Over the phone wasn't working. He was acting like a child, and that couldn't last. In the meantime, though, she had to stay clear of Theo. Which meant she wouldn't be leaving the Blu because while she'd done okay controlling herself around him last night, she couldn't trust herself for long. He was irresistible. All the heroes she wrote about were mainly based on him, not that she'd ever admit that, but it was true.

He was the one who got away.

Or better yet, the one who was thrown in jail for drug trafficking.

Which may have been good for her at the time.

Gen had needed those two weeks with him. To feel that rush, to know what she wanted but could never have. Her dad had made sure of that with his threats of not paying for school if she waited around for Theo the way she'd wanted. Even with her dad telling her Theo wasn't the one for her, it took a long time for her to accept that. When she graduated college and came home, seeing Montgomery for the first time since they were kids, she could glimpse a little bit of Theo in him. Just a bit and that alone had her giving Montgomery a chance. He was comfortable, he was easy, and he worked so much that she really didn't have to do much but write, which was what she wanted.

But then that all went to hell in a handbasket the moment he asked her to marry him.

What was she doing?

The tears ran down the sides of her face, emotion suffocating her from the inside. Seeing Theo, fighting with Montgomery. It was such a mess. Two weeks ago, her life was easy, but that wasn't the case anymore. But did she even want easy? Where was her sense of adventure, her bad streak? She was wild during college, but that all ended the moment she entered into a relationship with Montgomery. That hadn't saddened her, she was older, she couldn't be a teen anymore. But was she really cut out to be the kind of woman a man came home to, who had dinner ready and the kids on perfect behavior? No, no, she wasn't.

It was over.

Squeezing her eyes shut, the tears still leaking out, she suspected she'd known this before she even came to Spring Grove. She may have always known, especially when they started fighting about her job. What had she done? Why was she dragging this out? Why did she really come here? Montgomery was right; she could have written at home, but she'd needed to come here. Why?

She wanted to say she had an answer, but she didn't.

She threw the pillow off her face and opened her eyes with a groan she was sure bounced off the walls. She needed food, she needed some water, and she needed to get to work. She had to finish, and then she had to go. She had to call everything off, she had to move out, she had to figure out her life. She owed all that to Montgomery. Pushing the blankets off her legs, she sat up slowly as the tears rolled down her face. Wiping her cheeks, she inhaled deeply and was about to get up when she noticed a tray positioned beside her bed with a carafe of water, some ice in a glass that had melted a little, along with two pieces of toast and cheese on a napkin.

Her brow perked as she reached for the water, dumping it over the ice before downing it. She hadn't realized she was so thirsty until she refilled her glass, drinking from it once more. Reaching for the toast, she ate it slowly as she thanked Delaney over and over again in her head. Gen didn't remember a lot from last night, especially after the puking episode. She'd blacked out, thankfully. But Delaney must have made sure she got into bed and tucked her in, like the good friend she was.

It was obvious from the look on Delaney's face that she hadn't expected to see Theo, which intrigued Gen. Why was that? Did he not live in town? Was he just passing through? There were so many questions circling her mind, but she knew they didn't matter. She couldn't care about those answers. She was in a relationship—yes, it was ending, but she wasn't that girl. She wouldn't cheat. So, really, what was she thinking about? She wouldn't even see him anymore. She knew that for a fact, and no matter how bad it sucked, she knew that was the way it had to be.

Stuffing the other piece of toast in her mouth, she headed for the bathroom to wash up and brush her teeth. She somehow found the strength to get in the shower. It was just what she needed. Getting out, she threw her hair in a wet bun and got dressed in a pair of shorts and a large tee. Grabbing the carafe and her glass, she sat down at her desk, opening her computer. She was on a mission, and she was going to get it done, damn it.

He felt so good. So damn good as he wrapped her body up in his thick arms. Her body was vibrating against his, his cock throbbing along the inside of her thigh as she let her head fall back to his chest, looking up at him. His face was flushed, his lips swollen from where she had bitten him and kissed the hell out of him. He was beautiful. Her forever. As his eyes met hers, she smiled at the uncertainty in his gaze. She knew he was nervous. She was his best friend's sister. But what Matt didn't know, and neither did Travis, was that Ashley had wanted Travis for a very long time. She wasn't the baby they both saw her as. She was a woman, and she had fantasies that starred Travis.

Closing her eyes as his lips slowly caressed her, she moved her hands down his hips to his thighs, her nails biting into his skin. His kisses became more demanding, his arms tightening around her. She wanted him. Again. And again. She didn't care that she had to be at work or that he had to go either. She didn't care about anything but him fucking her.

"I want you inside of me," she whispered against his mouth. His eyes were hooded as he shook his head.

"Angel, we both have places to be."

"I want you inside of me," she said again, more sternly, moving her hand between her legs, stroking him along her thigh. "Don't you want me?"

His jaw went taut, his eyes darkening as he took in a quick breath. "That's not fair."

"When do I ever play fair?"

He was breathing heavily, but all she could do was grin at him. She loved him. God, she did, and she knew that they might not work, that he would more than likely sabotage them, but until then, she was going to get her fill of him. She went to turn, but his arms wouldn't allow her to. "No, Ash, we gotta go."

Her eyes darkened. "I want you to fuck me."

"You're killing me. I can't be late, and neither can you."

"I don't care, Travis. I want you inside of me. Now."

She challenged him with her eyes, and when a slow grin moved over his lips, her heart leaped up into her throat. She thought he was going to kiss her, slowly lay her down, but boy was she wrong. Slamming her down onto the bed, face first, he held her down with his hand as he positioned his cock at her entrance. "Want me to fuck you, huh?"

She was breathless as she moved her face out of the covers, trying to look up at him, but his hand was holding her square in the middle of the back. "Yes. Now."

He groaned loudly as he slammed into her, so hard, she cried out. But not in pain. In total and unbelievable pleasure. He was so big, so thick, and she wanted nothing more than to be fucked until she couldn't walk. His hand held her at his hip, holding her so tightly it burned as he continued to slam into her, over and over again. Each time felt deeper, and she swore she would never again feel what Travis made her feel. She could feel him throbbing—he was almost there—but she also knew he wasn't wearing a condom.

"Finish off in my ass."

He stilled, his breathing so fast as he squeezed her hip. Pulling out of her, he smacked her ass hard, causing her to cry out. He took her by her hips, pulling her up on her knees, which confused her for maybe a moment before his mouth was on her ass, running his tongue along her asshole and vagina. Crying out from the sheer pleasure, she dug her fingers into the sheets as his fingers bit into her ass.

"I can't handle you," she cried out as he spat on her anus.

"Oh, baby, I'm not even done."

His words vibrated her soul, and when he joined her on the bed, his thighs lining up with hers, she held her breath as he pushed his lubed-up cock inside of her ass, groaning with every inch that disappeared inside of her. "Mercy—"

Fuck.

Closing her eyes, she shook her head. Why was she writing that? She laughed. Why did she even ask that? She knew why. Pressing the delete button on her keyboard, she took the word out before she reached for her cup, only to discover it was empty.

"Damn it."

Looking back at the carafe of water, she noticed she had drunk it all too. So she grabbed it, heading downstairs to refill it so she could get back to work. The house was quiet as she walked down the stairs, and when she glanced out the window on her way to the kitchen, she noticed Delaney's car wasn't there. She'd probably thought Gen would be sleeping all morning, which was a fair assessment, but what Delaney didn't know was that Gen had a plan. A plan she was going to stick to.

Reaching the kitchen, she went to the fridge to get some of the filtered water. As it filled, she looked around the large kitchen that was decorated with roosters, and she smiled. She had bought a lot of these roosters for Ms. Neil, and it made her happy the new owner had kept them. Then she wondered if they'd mind if she took one, just to remember Ms. Neil by. Man, she missed that lady. Gen was convinced Ms. Neil would know exactly what to do about Montgomery. Even though Gen knew she had to end it, she wasn't sure how that was going to happen. Montgomery was a very proud man; he wouldn't take her breaking up with him lightly. Which sucked.

Sighing heavily as the water finished, she pulled the carafe back just as she heard, "Mercy me, I'm surprised you're vertical."

The words ran up her spine as she turned slowly, her eyes widening at the sight of Theo leaning against the island like he belonged there. A grin sat on those devilish lips, his eyes bright and full of actual surprise. "I was convinced you'd sleep all day. Oh good, your eye didn't blacken." When his grin grew, his eyes dropping to her shirt and shorts, he smirked. "Nice."

Her eyes widened more when she realized she was wearing her shortest shorts and a shirt with no bra. She'd taken her hair out of its bun, and the damp strands brushed across her shoulders. Exasperation flowed through her body as she glared over at him. "What in the hell are you doing?"

He gave her a dry look. "Well, at this particular moment, I'm admiring your thighs, but I was fixing the stove. It went out last night."

She pursed her lips. "Don't look at my thighs."

He shot her a cocky look. "Hey, they're on display, darling."

"Don't call me darling!" she added and he laughed. "And don't say *mercy!*"

That made him laugh harder before he shrugged, so carefree and not even the least bit concerned he was driving her wild. "Free country."

She glared. "So, you fix things around here? When are you leaving? I've got work to do and wanted to go to the porch, but not while you're here."

He scoffed. "What the hell did I do?"

"You exist."

"Hey, you liked my existence when I was carrying you up those stairs and tucking you into bed."

"You did not!"

"I did," he laughed, his eyes blazing blue. "And you loved puking on me, which by the way, you owe me for laundry. Those were my favorite pair of jeans."

"You have like nine of the same pair!"

"So?"

"So!" she yelled, her body shaking with annoyance and maybe a little lust, but that was probably from the hot love scene she was just writing. "When are you going to be gone?"

He just shook his head, feigning hurt as he pressed his hand to his chest. "Good golly, Genny, I never thought I'd hear ya want me to leave."

She pressed her lips together because the truth was, she didn't want him to leave. But that was beside the point! She had to stay away from him. "I don't know what you're implying, but I am engage—"

"Please. If you gave two shits about your *engagement,* you'd already be gone by now."

That took her aback, and she insisted, "I have a book to finish!"

"That you could finish at home if you wanted. You don't want to be there. You want to be here, which is why you haven't left."

She shook with anger. "You don't know shit!"

He just grinned at her. "I know a lot."

"Not about me."

He shrugged. "I know I'd give my left nut to suck on that right nipple."

She gasped, glancing down where her nipple was, in fact, betraying her. She looked back up at him, her eyes wild with rage while her body filled with something she would not give an identity to. "Go away!"

He just laughed. "No can do, darling. I have work to do."

"Then get it done. And leave so I can work. And then leave town."

His eyes darkened, and in a low voice, he said, "You don't want me to leave, we both know that. Don't worry, when you figure that out, you can always find me."

He pushed off the counter as she glared at him. "I don't want to find you."

He just smiled back at her. "Just the same, this is where I'll be." When he hooked his thumb to Ms. Neil's old room, her eyes grew larger.

"Huh? Why would you be there?"

His grin was unstoppable. "Because this, darling, is my place."

And just like that, Gen saw her so-called plan implode.

CHAPTER 10

G awking at Theo, Gen couldn't believe what she was hearing.

"You lie."

He made a disgruntled face. "Why would I lie about that?"

"Why would you buy this place? This is my place. I love this place!"

He looked away, a soft chuckle leaving his lips as he nodded. "I know."

Flabbergasted, she threw her hand up. "What?"

He looked back to her, his eyes locking with hers, and chills rushed down her spine. "I know this is your place, and when Old Lady Neil died, I knew I wanted it."

"Why! You aren't an inn-runner person."

"An innkeeper? I thought you were the smart one here."

"I'm flustered!"

He shot her a sneaky grin. "Aww, do I make you flustered?"

"No! Ugh!" she yelled, setting the carafe on the island before she dropped it. Striking her hips, she glared at him. "This isn't what you wanted. You wanted to be a master distiller up at McElroy's."

His lips quirked. "You remember that?" Her heart was slamming in her chest as she just stared at him with what she was sure was a completely irrational and confused look. When he realized she wasn't going to answer him, he scoffed. "McElroy will hire anyone who needs a job, but he won't let some convicted drug trafficker be a master distiller, darling. No matter how long he's known me." She could only blink as he held her gaze. "I worked up there for a long time. I love it, and I do miss it, but no one wanted this place, and Ms. Neil didn't have anyone to take it over, so I decided to."

"You were here?"

His brow rose. "What?"

"You were here in this town? For how long?"

"Forever, except when I was in jail."

Her eyes widened. "I've come back, I've visited, and I've never seen you or even heard about you. Everyone is so tight-lipped when it comes to you."

He grinned. "Aw, you asked for me?"

"Theo! What the hell?"

He swallowed visibly as he looked away. "What, Genny? I almost ruined your life. Why would you even want to see me?"

She knew she should have said she didn't, she should have gone right upstairs, but she didn't move, her eyes trained on his. "You did not. I can't believe I was here and I never saw you. I came back every summer during college, then every spring after that—"

"And then you went on hiatus for four years."

She looked away. "We got engaged. He didn't want me coming up here anymore."

That made Theo laugh. "Is my big brother a jealous man?"

"Do you care?" she bit back, her heart out of control to the point where she felt as if she was going to pass out.

"I don't." He wore his hatred for his father and his brother like a badge of honor. There was no love lost between the three men, and everyone was just fine with that. She understood it; they treated him like the bastard he technically was, but sometimes it was a little too much. She felt awful for Theo, which was the main reason she'd left with him when he asked her to. It was so long ago. So much had changed, and she just didn't understand it.

"So why now?" she found herself whispering. "Why now am I allowed to know you still live here? Why'd you have everyone lie to me? What the hell?"

He cleared his throat. "Well, I was hoping you'd be back that spring after you left. I wanted to meet up then—"

"Why? You had plenty of chances before."

He nodded, and for the first time, gone was the playful grin, replaced by an almost shy one. Her eyes narrowed. Shy and Theo Hudson didn't go in the same sentence. Clearing his throat, he met her baffled gaze. "Genevieve, come on. I was scum back then, a boy with no clue what I was doing except that I wanted to be able to take care of my momma and you. That blew up in my face, my pride was shattered, and I was embarrassed. I couldn't expect you to wait around for me."

Her mouth fell open more, and she gawked at him as she shook her head. "But I did! For four fucking years, I came back here like clockwork, and I never saw you. No one told me shit."

"You shouldn't have. I wasn't worth it then."

"That's my opinion to have. We had no closure whatsoever. You just left, and I knew nothing. I wanted to see you, make sure you were okay. Jesus, Theo, I was in love with you." As soon as the words flew out of her mouth, she covered it just as quickly. She was in complete disbelief that she had said that. It was true, but still. It was so long ago, and it hurt, all of it. How he was taken away, how there was no contact, no fucking closure. She slowly opened her eyes to find him watching her. He was standing, tucking his hands into his pockets as his gaze met her clouded one. She hadn't expected the tears, but could she really be surprised by them?

Yeah, it was only two weeks so many years ago. But in those two weeks, she fell so hard for the boy who was now a man, standing across a kitchen island from her. She had been convinced no one would ever come close to him in her heart. They hadn't.

Montgomery was a different kind of love, a controlled, comfortable one, but the love she had for Theo was completely uninhibited. It was crazy, and she missed it. But this could not happen. She wasn't sure what *this* was, but she could see it in his eyes. He wanted *this*.

She let out a sigh with a shake of her head. "I gotta go work."

He didn't answer for a moment, and when she reached for the carafe, his hand covered hers, stopping her dead in her tracks. "Or we could eat some lunch, catch up."

She shook her head, biting hard into her lip. "Theo, I am engaged."

"I'm not asking you to do me on the table. Though, I would enjoy very much covering your body in the strawberry glaze I made for the cheesecake. Eat it right off those perky tits of yours."

Gasping, she moved her hand out from under his, smacking his hand. "Theodore!"

"What? It's true. Wanna taste it? It's sugary sweet, would go amazing with those thick as honey hips," he said, his eyes sparkling with mischief as they roamed across her waist.

Throwing her hands up, she groaned loudly before snatching the carafe from him. "No! I am engaged," she said once more, and she tried so hard to ignore the fact that her insides were throbbing. Slickness gathering between her thighs. Damn it, Theo! "You don't flirt with engaged women. It's tasteless."

"I apologize."

"You do not!"

He shrugged, that damn grin back. "You're right, I don't."

She went to stomp away, but he stopped her, his hand grabbing her arm and causing the water to splash up on him and all over his shirt. He jumped in surprise, and she scoffed. "Karma is a bitch."

He gave her a look as he chuckled softly. "If karma is after me for flirting with you, Genevieve Stone, then I'm okay with that because I won't stop."

She inhaled deeply, which was a total mistake because all she did was cloud her senses with his spicy and naughty cologne. "Theo, please don't. It's not right."

His head dropped a bit, and she swore he was gonna kiss her. She realized she wasn't going to stop him, and guilt rushed over her. But then he was talking. "I just want you to know that I wouldn't ever flirt with you if I knew this engagement was real, that you intended to leave here and marry him. I would respect you, even him, but that's not the case. You left your home for a reason, and while it may not have been me, I'm here."

Her eyes stayed locked with his as she slowly shook her head. "Let me go, please."

The grin was in place as he let her go, but he didn't move, and before she could get away, he whispered, "I loved you back then, Gen. I loved you more than I knew what to do with."

She gasped, looking up at him in total disbelief. "Theo. Stop."

"I never stopped."

Her heart dropped, and before she could stop him, his mouth caught hers in a quick kiss. When he pulled back, his eyes burning into hers, she wasn't sure what happened. Something snapped then, could have been her sanity or his, because his arms were around her, his mouth pressing into hers as the carafe fell from her hands, crashing to the ground. He picked her up off the ground, and her legs went around his waist as he pressed her into the wall. She was soon kissing him just as hard as he was kissing her. His lips were perfection, his arms so tight around her. He tasted so damn good, strawberries and a hint of cigarettes, the taste driving her mad. His tongue found hers, and she groaned loudly against his mouth as her center throbbed against his stomach. Bunching up her hair in one hand, he took her breast in his other hand as her nails dug into his shoulders. Their kisses were out of control and sloppy. It was so right. It felt just like she remembered, and the lust was so overpowering she almost forgot who she was.

Almost.

Tearing her mouth from his, she shook her head as she pushed him back, her feet coming to the ground. "Theo. Stop. Really."

He eyed her, but when she pushed him once more, he took a step back, his hands up. "Genevieve—"

"No. Stop," she said, shaking her head. With that, she went up the stairs, taking them two at a time until she was in the safety of her room. When she slammed the door shut, she leaned into it as she took in her whole room. He had done this. She knew he had, and she wanted to enjoy the fluttery feeling his thoughtfulness left her with, but she couldn't.

Because she was pretty sure she had just cheated on Montgomery.

CHAPTER 11

Digging her toes into the sand, she looked out on the lake as her phone hung in her fingers. She was done writing for the day and knew she didn't have much left to go in the book. She wasn't sure how she'd gotten anything done when she could still taste Theo all over her mouth, but she had. If she was honest, the sex Travis and Ashley had just had for a chapter and half was some of the hottest she had ever written. But she felt dirty. Awful. She wasn't a cheater, but she was pretty sure that little kissing session she had with Theo in the kitchen was cheating at its finest.

And the thing that bothered her the most was that she almost didn't regret it. She regretted it because she was with someone, someone she did respect. But she didn't regret it because for the first time in months, hell years, she'd felt something. Something wild and amazing. Her soul sang and it was beyond beautiful, but she knew it was wrong. She glanced at her phone, hoping that Montgomery had texted her back. Alas, he hadn't.

She didn't understand how her life had gotten so crazy. She also didn't like when Theo had said she had come there for a reason.

Was it really to get away from Montgomery? Was she using the excuse of writing as a ploy to get away? Was she running?

Shit. She was.

When someone sat down beside her, she jumped a bit until she realized it was Delaney. "Hey."

"Hey, girl, surprised to see you alive."

Gen's lips quirked, though she didn't smile. "Yeah, I'm alive."

"Hey, you don't have a black eye. That's good."

"Yeah," Gen said, though she didn't care.

"Why you out here alone? Isn't the cat out of the bag?"

She nodded, looking at Delaney. "Why didn't you tell me?"

"I promised him I wouldn't," she answered simply.

"Why would he make you promise that?"

Delaney exhaled heavily and then shrugged. "Well, back when you used to visit, I did it because he was my cousin's best friend. Now I do it because I got into some serious trouble with this guy online."

Gen's brows drew in. "What do you mean?"

She shrugged, shaking her head. "I met up with this guy. He seemed okay online, but when we got to the restaurant down in Elmont, I started getting a weird vibe from him. I went to the bathroom, and when I came out, he was waiting there. Scared the shit out of me, but he said he was only wanting to make sure I made it to the table okay. But it felt off, ya know? So when we got back to the table, I texted my cousin. He didn't answer, and I started to panic, so I texted Theo. He came right on up there, and when the guy started freaking out because Theo came to get me, Theo popped him dead in the nose." She paused, inhaling as she looked out into the lake. "So when he bought the Blu, he asked me never to tell you, that he wanted to do it. So I did. I could have been overreacting about the guy, but nonetheless, Theo came to my rescue."

Gen took in the profile of Delaney's face and smiled. "I wasn't mad."

"Oh, I know, but I owe you an explanation. I mean, we are friends."

Gen nodded. "We are."

They shared a smile. "So, friend, how is everything? You look... confused. Yeah, confused."

Gen laughed as Delaney grinned over at her. "Things are nuts."

"What? You're on vacation. How are things nuts?"

Gen bit her lip as she shook her head. "Theo kissed me, and I kissed him back."

"Damn," Delaney sang, and then she was counting on her fingers. "You knew about him for what, twelve hours, and already attacked him? I'm impressed. Not surprised, but impressed."

Gen rolled her eyes. "Don't be. I'm still engaged."

"So? You're breaking it off, right?"

"Probably, but still, it's disrespectful and rude. I'm not that girl."

"Everyone knows that, but sometimes things just happen."

"I should have controlled myself."

Delaney giggled. "I mean, Theo ain't nothing to roll an eye at. He's always been a tall glass of heaven."

Gen scoffed. "I know, but I know better. He wouldn't want that done to him, and now I'm doing it to Montgomery."

Delaney shrugged. "I get what you're saying, and you're right. So just tell Montgomery."

"He won't answer the phone."

Delaney gasped. "Jesus, you were really gonna tell him?"

"Yes!" Gen laughed. "I was in the wrong. I didn't want to tell him over the phone or break it off like that, but I can't let it go that long, ya know? It will be like I'm hiding it."

Delaney shook her head. "You're a good woman, Gen."

"I feel like junk."

Delaney shrugged. "That's the whiskey."

That made Gen laugh as she rolled her eyes. "I can't believe Theo's here."

"Believe it. He's been waiting for you."

"Another thing I find hard to believe."

"Eh, it's true," Delaney said with a grin, but then she clapped her hands together. "So, what are you doing right now?"

"Nothing, I guess, since Montgomery won't answer my calls or texts."

"Cool, come with me. Randy Goosemen's house just came up for rent, across the lake from my mawmaw's."

Gen made a face. "You're gonna move out?"

"I'm thirty, it's time."

"Delaney."

"Okay, she's pissing me off, and I'm gonna scare her. She'll see us looking. Come on." As they got up, Gen laughed as she shook her head at her friend. She was pretty sure Delaney wouldn't move out of her mawmaw's house until the day she moved in with her husband. "And then afterward, we can head to the town square for the pre-Fourth party."

Gen stopped her. "Will there be whiskey?"

Delaney nodded. "Yes, but none for you. Everyone is still talking about how you upchucked all over Theo."

Gen's face warmed, but she wasn't surprised nor bothered by everyone talking about her.

That was the charm of small-town living.

⚜

WHEN THEY REACHED THE LITTLE ONE-BEDROOM CABIN THAT sat right along the banks of Kentucky Lake, Gen gasped loudly. "Oh, Delaney, this is gorgeous."

"It is, isn't it?" Delaney threw open the door and got out, and Gen did the same as she continued to take in the little home. She knew it was only one bedroom because that's what Delaney had said, but she almost didn't believe her. It was so small and cute, almost like a studio apartment. She wasn't sure, but she had to find out. After she ran to catch up with Delaney, they went in, and she oohed and aahed some more. To her surprise, the inside was bigger than the outside let on.

The living room was adorable, with space for probably just a couch or maybe a chair and nice big desk. The kitchen was small, but still had everything a girl would need to cook. The bathroom was adjacent to the one bedroom, which was slightly bigger than the living room but had a beautiful patio off it, looking out at the lake. It was spectacular.

"I think you should live here."

Delaney laughed. "Nope, don't need to. Plus, why move when I pay nothing where I'm at?"

"Because this place is breathtaking." A smile sat on Gen's face as she exhaled loudly. "Look, you can sit here and—"

"What, fart? I don't do anything cool."

She gave Delaney a dry look and shook her head. "I'd write. Right here." She ran her hand down the kitchen table. "Or on the patio. Either-or."

"Then you move here."

That made Gen laugh really hard. "Yeah, right. I couldn't."

"Why not?" Delaney asked, and Gen laughed some more.

"What? Be real, I couldn't live here. I have a life in DC."

Delaney held her hands out to Gen. "That's about to end once you call off this thing with Montgomery." Gen's smile slowly faded as she realized Delaney was speaking the truth. "I'm sure I can get them to hold it for you. Or hell, put a deposit down, and it's yours."

Gen could only blink. She hadn't even thought about what she would do when she ended things with Montgomery. She knew she would be asked to leave the house, with good reason, but would she leave DC altogether? Her mom and dad. Her friends... Well, obviously she didn't have many since no one had called her since she left, but still. Crap.

Before she could answer Delaney, though, her phone rang. Pulling it out of her pocket, she found it was Montgomery.

"Excuse me," she said as she went out onto the patio, shutting the door as she answered. "Hello."

"You called," he said, very rushed and monotone.

"I did. I wanted to apologize for last night."

He said nothing. She could hear him typing, but that was it. "Okay."

"Okay," she said slowly. "I'm sorry."

"I don't think it's right that my fiancée is out drinking without me."

"You drink without me all the time, and I don't complain."

"Because I'm with colleagues, friends."

"I was with friends."

He let out an annoyed breath as he snapped, "Whatever. What are you doing now? What did you need?"

This was a shitshow, she decided. "I'm looking at this adorable little cabin with Delaney." When Gen was met with silence, she asked, "Hello?"

"Looking at a house, huh?"

"Yeah, it's really pretty. It's on the lake, only one bedroom, but it's adorable—"

"So is that where I'm sending your stuff?"

She paused. "Excuse me?"

"What, Gen? It's a pretty simple question. It's obvious you've moved on, looking at houses and all that. Was that a lead-in to let me know we're done? That you're calling everything off?"

Taking in a shaky breath, she shook her head as she shut her eyes. "I'm with Delaney, she's looking at the house." He didn't answer back, and she rolled her eyes. "I don't understand what your deal is and why you assume the worst about me. But you know what? Yeah, I'm done."

He scoffed. "I'm not the least bit surprised."

"Wow, no?"

"Nope, I knew you were done the moment you left. So what, you're fucking around on me?"

"I would never," she insisted, but then she pressed her lips together. "I'm not you. I don't fuck people with I'm with someone."

"Whatever you have to say to make yourself feel better, Genevieve."

"What the hell, Montgomery—"

"Nope, nothing else to say. Send me the address, and I'll ship your stuff."

"Wait," she demanded, anger vibrating through her body.

She fully expected to hear a dial tone, but instead, she heard, "What?"

"Are you fucking around on me again?"

"Please," he laughed. "I don't have the time."

"I find it real fishy that you're okay with this. That you're just so dismissive."

"Maybe I've been done too," he answered, and it was like a slap in the face. When the line went dead, she dropped her phone, tucking it into her pocket as she looked out at the lake.

What the fuck was happening?

When the patio door opened, Delaney popped her head out. "Hey, you ready?" Gen turned, looking at her, and Delaney's brows pulled together. "Whoa, you okay? What happened?"

"We broke up," she said, and just like that, her phone started ringing off the hook. It was her mother, then Verna, then her father.

"Jesus, give me that," Delaney demanded before taking it and turning it off.

"He didn't even care. He wasn't upset or anything. Maybe he was cheating on me?"

"Probably," Delaney said, tucking Gen's phone into her back pocket. "Once a cheater, always a cheater. Now, come on, let's go to the pre-Fourth."

But Gen shook her head. "No, maybe I should go on back to the Blu."

"Nope, I'm not gonna let you sit at the house and wallow over this. You came here for vacation. Let's party!"

But Gen still wouldn't smile. "Delaney, my five-year relationship just ended, and I think I'm more upset than he is. I need to analyze this a bit."

"Tomorrow. Let's go have a blast tonight."

Gen swallowed back the sob that was threatening to escape. While she had wanted this, to be done, she also wanted some kind of sadness from him. Hadn't he ever loved her? Was he fucking around on her? Damn it, why was this such a mess? When she glanced up, Delaney's eyes were pleading. Gen knew if she did just go home, she'd cry herself to sleep. Delaney was right. She was there to have a good time and finish her book.

And she was done writing for the day.

"Let's go."

CHAPTER 12

The so-called pre-Fourth party was basically an excuse for everyone to meet up, eat, and drink. A time for the locals to enjoy the festivities before all the tourists showed up. The tiny square was packed with the whole town, Gen was convinced, as she pushed through everyone, saying hi and hugging those who recognized her. Some even asked for her to sign something, which she found incredibly sweet. When she was asked by the librarian of the town, Ambrosia McElroy, who was also Old Man McElroy's youngest child, to come sign Zoe Jayne books at the library, she found herself saying yes. It made her laugh, though. She didn't even know what she was doing with her life, but she was making arrangements? She was insane. Her life was insane, and she knew her mom and dad were probably still calling her. She'd need to answer them. Tomorrow. Tomorrow would be a good day for that.

With her arm hooked through Delaney's, Gen made her way through the crowd to where Delaney said everyone would be waiting. And they were—her mawmaw, her cousin, Holden, their great-aunt, Jackie, along with Theo. Gen stopped suddenly, tapping Delaney's arm. "Don't tell Theo."

Delaney paused. "Huh? What?"

"Don't tell Theo about me breaking it off with Montgomery."

She eyed Gen, but soon Delaney nodded her head. "Of course."

They were almost to where everyone was sitting when Theo saw her. His eyes met hers, and a little grin pulled at his lip as he drank her in. It was so overwhelming, the pounding of her heart, that she had to look away. But when she did, her gaze met that of Old Man McElroy.

"Genevieve Stone, why haven't I seen you up at my distillery?"

Letting go of Delaney, Gen wrapped her arms around the big man as he gobbled her up in a hug. He was a very large man, tall and round with bushy red brows and even brighter red hair. His nose was always red, from sunburn probably, but his personality was bigger than the town. Gen adored him. "I may not have made it up there, but I've drunk a lot of your whiskey since coming here."

He laughed, a big, booming noise, as he let her go. "That doesn't count! I want you in my distillery, on my land, drinking with me. Ya hear?"

"I hear you," she laughed and he smiled.

"Now, girl, you know I got three sons and a daughter. So if you're looking for someone, I have both sexes."

Gen laughed harder, shaking her head. "Thank you, but I'm fine."

Suddenly, out of the corner of her eye, she saw Theo getting up and heading to the bar. She watched him, her body catching on fire as she shook her head in disgust at herself.

She was pathetic.

But Old Man McElroy must have seen her because, with a roll of his eyes, he whistled loudly and boomed, "Still held up on that boy, I see? I guess, when it's love, it's love."

Gen laughed nervously. "No, not at all."

"Don't lie to me, sugar. I know a woman in love. I've been married sixty-two years. Haven't we, Shirley?"

"We sure have," his lovely wife yelled back with a grin on her face. "Hey there, Genevieve."

Gen waved before she looked back at Old Man McElroy. "Let's both agree to disagree, okay? And tell me when you want me to come up."

"Anytime! I'm always there. Hell, if you don't want me to show you around, have Theo. He knows that place better than my oldest boy, for sure," he said, shaking his head. "If that boy would come home and follow in my footsteps, life would make sense. Instead, he wants to be a vet." He laughed loudly. "Who wants to be shit on by animals all day?"

Gen just smiled, unsure what to say. She remembered when his oldest, she couldn't remember his name, first said he wanted to leave. People around here treated him like he'd basically died. "And in Lexington? Who would actually want to leave this beautiful place? Our Spring Grove. Hell, you know that, right, Genevieve? You never wanna leave."

She didn't. She loved it here.

"Hey, Gen, come on," Delaney called to her, and Gen nodded before looking back up at Old Man McElroy.

"I'll see you soon, okay?"

"All right, sugar. Have a great night."

"You too," she called as she walked away, trying to get past the crowd, but it was tight. When she finally got through, Delaney was sitting with Holden, as Jackie and Mawmaw seemed to be in one heated discussion.

"I did sleep with him!"

"You did not!"

"Yes, I did. 1972!"

"No, I did in 1978."

"Who are they arguing about?"

"Old Man McElroy," Delaney said dryly, shaking her head. "They do this every time they drink his whiskey."

Gen made a face as Holden rolled his eyes. Gen was confused though, and with a tip of her chin toward where Old Man McElroy was, she mentioned, "He just said he's been married for like sixty something years."

Holden laughed. He was a very tall man. His father, wherever he was, was almost seven feet tall from what they all said. Holden was thick with muscle and worked hard over at the distillery. He was a good old boy, messy brown hair, big brown eyes, and nice lips. There wasn't much about him that was extraordinary, except that his mom tried to kill him when he was two, which was why Mawmaw had raised him. He was a sweet guy, though, real good to Delaney and her older sister, and also Theo's best friend. Holden had told Theo not to get involved with the people who had given him the drugs, but at the time, Theo wanted the money. "He's only like sixty. And even so, everyone knows he used to get around on old Shirley."

Gen made a face. "That's sad."

"Hell, she was doing it too!" Delaney added, and Gen rolled her eyes.

"Crazy."

"I should have been Mrs. McElroy."

"Nope. I should have been."

The two old ladies who favored each other continued to glare. Gen was a bit worried a fight would break out, but then five beers appeared and Theo said, "Or maybe both of y'all were supposed to be. Like sister wives or something."

"Yes!" Holden agreed, taking a beer and tapping it to Theo's. "Exactly. Good Lord."

"Exactly," Delaney agreed, rolling her eyes.

"Maybe, but I would have been the one he banged every night," Mawmaw said, and both Holden and Delaney gagged as Gen just laughed.

Leaning toward her, Theo laid a kiss to her cheek. "You're damn right, Pearl. The only one."

"I never did like you, boy!" Jackie yelled, smacking him, but he got away, laughing as Pearl just beamed. Sitting down beside Gen, he tipped his beer to her and then took a long pull. She watched as he drank quickly, his Adam's apple moving with the action. For some reason, it turned her on. She wanted to taste his neck, to touch him. But she couldn't.

"Went and checked out Randy Goosemen's house that's for rent," Delaney announced, which cut off all conversation for Pearl, who scooted closer to listen. "I love the patio. You were right, Holden."

"Told ya. It's a great house, and his grandson will give it to ya for cheap. I'm gonna rent the one at the bottom of the hill, on the other side of the town."

"You're moving out of Spring Grove?" Jackie gasped. "Why would you do that, boy?"

"My front yard will be Spring Grove, my back will be Lynchmount. I'll be only four minutes instead of two from Mawmaw's house. It's fine," he explained, but Jackie wasn't convinced.

"Why don't you move into the new house?"

"'Cause it's farther from Mawmaw, and Del wants it."

"No, she doesn't," Mawmaw said, shaking her head. "She just wants to piss me off."

Delaney snickered but covered it with a cough. "I am not. I'm moving."

That threw them into another argument that had Gen rolling her eyes. Leaning on the table with her elbows, she took a pull of her beer. The town was so beautiful at that moment. Lights hung everywhere, illuminating the whole area. The local restaurants were open for people to take their food out and eat. The dance floor was full of children dancing and having a blast. Everything was just perfect, except for the fact that she wasn't wallowing over Montgomery.

Instead, she was wondering if Theo was watching her. Which wasn't right. She should be heartbroken, unsure what to do about her newfound single life. In a way, she was, but at the same time, she wasn't. She wanted to know if Montgomery had been cheating on her and why he didn't care that she had broken it off with him. But other than that, she didn't care. It made no sense. Five fucking years. How could someone seem so unaffected by breaking up with someone after that long?

She was still affected after ten years of being apart from Theo.

She should really consider taking into account why she wasn't facedown in her bed crying over the loss of her five-year relationship. Why did she let it go on so long? She should have known. When the sex started to be expected instead of exciting, she should have known.

Damn it.

"You look pretty tonight,"

Gen's breath caught as she looked over at Theo, who was, in fact, watching her. "Excuse me?"

He scoffed, shaking his head as his lips moved along the top of his bottle. "Ya heard me just fine."

She eyed him and then looked away. "Thank you. It's just a dress."

"That's driving me damn well insane."

She inhaled sharply, biting the inside of her cheek as she tried to listen to Mawmaw and Delaney go at it. It was stupid, though, and she couldn't help wanting to turn to Theo and asking him a billion questions about his life now. She knew it would be shitty of her, but man, she wanted it so bad. She looked over at him to find him still staring at her, a grin on his lips as he ran the tip of his bottle along his bottom lip.

"You know what you need?"

Her brows rose to her hairline. "What?"

"Someone to take you dancing," he decided, placing his beer down and standing up. He was wearing a nice button-down shirt, a light blue color that set off his eyes. His jeans were dark and worn, of course, frayed at the bottom, meeting his boots in perfect harmony. His hair was brushed to the side, his beard so big and bushy. She was still on the fence about it, but boy, was it nice when they were kissing earlier. "You wanna dance with me?"

His words hit her like a sledgehammer. "Oh, no, I don't dance."

"Sure ya do," he said, and then she felt all eyes on her.

"No—"

"Now, go on, Genevieve. A good dance will do the soul good," Mawmaw said, giving her a wink.

"And he's a hunk," Jackie added, and Gen snorted at that.

"Plus, if you don't, he'll just harass you until you do," Delaney said, and Gen looked up at Theo to see him nodding.

"I sure as hell will. Now come on," he demanded, holding his hand out for her once more. She usually hated dancing, but she took his hand. Her heart sped up in her chest as he led her through the crowd and to the dance floor as "Girl Crush" by Little Big Town filled the speakers. Spinning her out, catching her off guard, he brought her in, and she went flat to his chest. Taking her hand in his, he intertwined their fingers as his other hand rested at the small of her back.

And then they were dancing.

Slowly.

Everything was on fire. Her fingers were numb, her lower back tingling, but all she could do was look into his eyes. His beautiful blue eyes that took away every rational thought. Licking his lips, he smiled as he moved them around the floor in time with everyone else. She wasn't doing the steps that apparently everyone knew, but she kept up, mostly because of him. He was almost carrying her.

She found herself asking, "Your girlfriend isn't here?"

He chuckled. "No girlfriend."

"Wife?"

"Nope."

"Boyfriend?"

That made his face break into a grin as he shook his head. "None of that either."

She nodded as she bit her lip. "So you've been working at the distillery all this time?"

"Yup. Working and hollering at the moon."

She rolled her eyes. "You're such a badass."

"I know," he said with a wink. "And you? Just writing?"

She looked away, nodding thoughtfully. "Yeah, lots of writing and then I'd go to events with Montgomery. But mostly writing."

He nodded, his face turning into a scowl when she mentioned Montgomery's name. "I've read all the books."

Her eyes widened, her heart stopping in her chest. "You have?"

"Yup. They're good."

Montgomery never read her books, and knowing that Theo had set her body on fire. "Oh. Thank you."

"Do you like your room?"

She swallowed hard. "I love it."

"I do too, it's my best room. Everyone loves it."

"You did that?"

"I did."

She just gazed up at him, rendered speechless as his eyes sparkled in the lights. When the song changed to "Losing Sleep" by Chris Young, everyone broke into their own little couples, dancing and being close with the person they were with. Theo and Gen just stayed in place by the corner of the dance floor, staring into each other's eyes. When he cleared his throat, she held her breath as he said, "I won't apologize for what I did earlier. I needed to kiss you, Genevieve Stone, but I will apologize for putting you in an uncomfortable position with Montgomery and all."

Her heart jumped in her throat. "Did you mean it?"

"Yes. I'm sorry, but not for kissing you—"

"No, not that," she said, cutting him off. "About still loving me."

The passion in his eyes intensified, if that was even possible, burning into hers. "I said it, didn't I?" he asked, those blue eyes flashing with promise. "When I say something, I mean it."

Her eyes burned with tears as she slowly shook her head in confusion. "What does that even mean, Theo?"

"It means I'm still very much in love with you."

She pushed him away, anger taking over as she shook her head. "Ten years, Theo! Ten."

"And I never stopped thinking of you and only you."

"Then why didn't you come after me? You had plenty of chances!"

He stepped toward her, his eyes intent on hers as he yelled, "Because I wasn't good enough for you. I wasn't rich enough. I was just some poor, bastard-ass kid. I wanted to be more. I wanted to be worthy of a woman as smart as you. As talented as you."

"That's not fair. You don't get to decide that! That's my decision. I cried for you, my heart was broken when you told me you weren't the one for me."

"I lied!"

She threw her hands up. "Well, the damage is done, isn't it? Ten years, we spent apart, and now you think we're just gonna jump back in? Is that what you want?"

"I want a fucking chance. Is that too much to ask for?"

"Was it too much to ask for when I needed some closure?"

He put his hand on his hip. "Because I didn't want you to have it. I wanted you to want me until I was able to give you the world."

"You were my world!" she yelled, ignoring the fact that everyone was staring at them. Her heart was almost coming out of her chest as she glared up at him. "I had it all. For years. And I kept coming back, looking for you, but you hid like a coward."

"And I'm sorry for that, but I wasn't ready," he said simply, and that's when the tears started to fall down her cheeks.

"Well, now I'm not. Great job, Theo."

With that, she left, with no clue how she'd ended up fighting with Theo at a party in the middle of the town square.

First, she'd puked on him, which got the town talking, and now, she'd fought with him.

No wonder Spring Grove never forgot Genevieve Stone.

CHAPTER 13

T ravis spat, blood spewing from his mouth into the grass. His face was bruised, and blood was coming from his nose. As Ashley moved closer, he looked away, running his hands down his face and then his pants to get rid of the blood.

Matt must have found out.

"Trav?"

"Go away, Ash."

"Are you okay?"

"I'm fine."

But she could see he wasn't. Sitting on the bench beside him, she reached out, trying to move his hand, but he flinched away, making her jump. "Let me see."

"No."

"Travis, let me help you. What happened?"

"You know what happened," he growled. "I told Matt."

Her stomach dropped. "You did what?"

"I told him."

"Why on earth would you do that? I told you I would."

He shook his head, blood flowing from his nose and onto the grass. "I needed to. He's my best friend."

"He's my brother."

"I don't care. I wanted to do it."

"Why?"

He inhaled a jagged breath, his whole body following the motion. When he finally turned, tears rushed to her eyes at the carnage that was his face. His nose was broken for sure, and he had a black eye and a busted chin. Crying out, she went to reach for him, but he stopped her. "We can't."

Her heart stopped. "What?"

"He said no. He said he'd kill me if I kept seeing you."

"No? What? Fuck him. It's my life. I want to be with you, Travis."

But he shook his head. "I'm not good enough."

"You are!" she cried, reaching for him and taking his hands. This time, he didn't fight. "Fuck what he said. You are mine. I love you, Travis. Do you love me?"

"I do."

"Then fuck what he thinks," she insisted, but he was shaking his head.

"You deserve someone good. Someone with a decent job, someone who can take care of you in ways I can't—"

"I want you."

Gen paused, reading what she had just written. It was good, not her best, but then she had locked herself in her room for the last three days. Only going down for snacks, and only when she knew Theo wasn't there. She found where he had parked his big ole green truck, so as soon as it left was when she'd go get food. It was pathetic and she knew she needed to face him, but his words were still rattling her.

Ten years. And he still loved her? Did she still love him? Seeing him blew her away. Knowing Theo was here, had been in this town as much as she had, shook her. Kissing him destroyed her. And dancing with him that night, being in his arms, looking up into his eyes, shit, it completed her. But she didn't know this man. She knew the boy. Oh, she could sing songs about crazy Theo Hudson at twenty, but who he was now, she wasn't sure.

And then there was Montgomery. She felt things weren't truly finished with him. She felt she needed to call and at least try to talk to him, explain herself, but there was radio silence on his end. Her mom was, of course, supportive. But she was also very upset since, apparently, Verna was trying to make Gen's father pay for the deposits that Verna had made. It was a mess and already the talk of the country club. While Gen knew she needed to go back to get her stuff and figure things out, she didn't want to. A part of her wanted to take Mont up on his offer to send her belongings here, but Lord, that would be such a cowardly thing to do. She should face him. Even though she didn't want to.

She wasn't sure how this all got so screwed up, but she knew it was her fault. Theo was right—hell, her mom was right when she said that Gen was running. When her mom showed her those pictures from the Blu, Gen was immediately gone. It was her way out, and as much as that was shitty, she didn't care. She was suffocating in DC, faking it. At least here, she was someone completely different. She was herself, she was alive, and she wasn't sure that was something she could give up. Not after having a taste of it again.

Closing her eyes, she let out a long breath and smiled.

This place was more her home than anywhere else was.

And she didn't feel the least bit guilty about that.

Looking out the window, she saw that it was a bright and airy summer day. She wanted so desperately to be outside enjoying it. Checking for Theo's truck, she noticed he wasn't home. She really needed to face him again, especially if she was considering living in beautiful Spring Grove. There was no way she wouldn't see him, mainly when he wanted to be seen. He was ruthless when he wanted something, she knew that. She remembered how he'd stood outside her house and wouldn't leave until her father let her go out to see him. Eleven hours, he'd stood there in the blistering heat. Her mom was feeding him and giving him sunscreen. It was pathetic, but he wouldn't leave. He wanted to talk to her.

She was pretty sure that had been the moment she'd fallen for him.

With a grin on her face, she gathered her laptop up and

headed downstairs. But when she reached the porch, she found it was too bright there for her laptop, so she settled for the breakfast nook table after opening all the windows and letting the breeze in. She poured herself some water and then grabbed some of the fruit Theo must have cut up, and she sat down to work. She was almost done with the book, would probably finish tomorrow, which was great since her deadline was the following week.

She was well into the chapter when the back door opened and Theo appeared with his arms full of bags. Surprised since she hadn't even heard his truck pull up, she bit into her lip. She looked back down at her laptop, but she had no clue what she was typing.

"Well, mercy, look who has emerged," he joked as he set everything on the island. "I was gonna come up there tonight if I didn't see you. I wasn't sure you were eating."

She wasn't going to answer him, but with an exhale, she nodded. "I am."

"Oh, good." She tried not to watch him, but it was hard. He was wearing those damn jeans that hugged his ass in such a way that had her drooling. His black tee was tight on his shoulders, and he was obviously hot since he was sweating down the back of it. He had his ball cap backward on his head as he started unloading the bags. When he turned, she quickly looked down as he laid a large, beautiful bouquet of sunflowers beside her laptop.

She glanced up at him, staggered, but he was turning back to the island without saying a word. Touching a petal, she said, "You didn't have to."

He looked over his shoulder. "I didn't. Those are for the vase."

She looked at the empty vase in the middle of the table and felt a little stupid. But when she looked up at him, he was grinning at her, and she knew he was messing with her. "Ass."

He laughed. "What? They're for the vase that I was gonna bring up to your room later."

A grin pulled at her lips, but she wouldn't allow them to curve. "Well, thank you."

"You're welcome." He moved with ease through the kitchen, putting things away and tidying as he went.

She should have ignored him, gone back to writing, but she couldn't. "Why aren't there any visitors? It's peak season."

He shrugged as he paused, the rag hanging loosely in his hands. "I wanted the house to ourselves while you were here."

Her brow perked. "Didn't you lose money?"

"Of course," he said with a shrug. "But to me, it's worth it."

Her heart skipped a beat. "It is?"

He just shot her a grin as he moved around the island, throwing things away. "Winning back the love of my life? Yeah, I'd say so."

He said it like it was a known thing, but it took away every breath Gen had inside of her. No one, and she meant no one, had ever been so blunt and so outright with what they were feeling except for Theo. He'd told her he loved her three days into knowing her, and while she'd thought he was insane, she found that she was foolish too because she had felt the same way. They just clicked.

"Oh."

He laughed at that as he threw the rag in the sink and then made his way toward her. She held her breath as he came around the table, grabbing the flowers and unwrapping them for the vase. He was close, his body big, and he smelled like heaven, so spicy. When he left to fill the vase with water, she found herself missing him, wanting him beside her, and that disgusted her. She would not jump into a new relationship. No matter who it was.

No matter how much she wanted Theo.

When he came back, he put the flowers in the water, and she expected him to walk away. Instead, he sat down in the chair beside her, leaning on his elbow, holding his chin in his hand as he asked, "So, what are we working on?" Her mouth parted, unsure what to say as she turned to glance at him. He was suddenly closer, reading what she had written as he nodded. "So what's going on? Who's Matt? Oh, her brother? Ack, oh, his best friend. Shit, lots going on here."

Her face broke into a grin as she met his gaze. "Travis, my hero, asked his best friend, her brother, if he can marry Ashley, the heroine."

"And Matt obviously said no and pounded his face?"

She was elated. Her heart sang as she nodded enthusiastically. "Yeah, but Ashley doesn't care what her brother says—"

"For good reason, she loves Travis. Is he shit?"

"Who, Travis? No, not at all. He's a good man, but his life has been hard."

"When is life not hard?" Theo laughed, leaning in closer to read. "He loves her a lot."

"He does, but he's worried he isn't good enough."

"I feel ya, Travis," he murmured, and she snickered a bit, which made his grin grow as he read. "Well, since they're tearing each other's clothes off, I think we're in the clear."

"Nowhere near. Matt will walk in as Travis is pounding her ass."

"Fucking fuck, you merciless asshole!" he joked and she laughed hard. Her whole body moved with the action as she leaned back. It felt good to laugh like that, and when it subsided, she found him watching her. "I love watching you laugh." She looked away, a grin pulling at her lips. "But can I suggest something?"

Her brow perked. "Sure?"

"Going from puss to ass and then back is gross. No female wants an infection from getting shit in her puss."

Gen's brows pulled together. "Oh. I hadn't thought that through yet."

"I mean, when you're getting pounded in the ass, and all of a sudden he transfers to the puss, you aren't like, fuck, shit is getting in my puss?"

Her cheeks warmed. "I don't know—"

"Wait, you haven't been pounded in the ass? You poser!"

Gen laughed. "I've watched plenty of porn."

"I mean, I love porn as much as the next guy, but that shit is fake and those women's vaginas are sick. All the time."

She laughed harder, shaking her head. "You're insane."

"I am," he agreed, pointing to the screen. "Have him going hard in that puss, his hands holding her, unable to get a grip on her because he wants her so damn bad. His mind will be going wild with love, lust, and the general need for all of her, every piece, until he is about to blow his load. Have him enter that sweet ass of hers, the feeling of completion coming over him as he fucks her until they both are quivering, and then he comes. He falls on top of her and holds her, promising he'd never do anything to lose her. That he'd love her for the rest of his days. That she is his and he is hers until they are six feet in the ground. That he loves her, and he'll never love anyone like he does her. He knows that for a fact."

Whoa.

When Theo looked over at her, Gen's body was tingling as she was gasping for breath. His eyes were dark with desire, his cheeks a little warm as he shot her a wink before he smiled widely at her. "Just a suggestion."

Breathless, Gen nodded. "It's a great one."

"Yeah, add in some of those fancy words you use, and I think it's a best seller."

She grinned. "Did you really read all my books?"

"Every single one."

Tears rushed to her eyes. "That's really sweet."

"Gotta support the girl who stole my heart, ya know," he answered, his hand resting on her thigh. She looked down at it and then up at him. He was right there, his mouth so close. All she had to do was take it, but she wasn't ready. She couldn't do this. She couldn't jump in with him when she didn't even know what the hell she was doing with her life. It wasn't fair to him. To her.

But before she could say that, he asked, "Hey, why don't we have dinner together tonight?"

She wasn't sure why she was surprised by that, but she was. "What?"

"Let me cook you dinner. You finish writing, I'll cook, and we'll eat on the dock." A grin pulled at his lips as his thumb moved up and down her thigh. "Just like that one time."

She laughed. "It wasn't dinner. It was cold-cut sandwiches."

"Which means whatever I cook will be a hundred times better."

She smiled. "This is true."

A silence fell between them, the only sounds those of birds tweeting and her body vibrating from the feel of his thumb on her skin. She knew she should say no, but she really didn't want to. She wanted to eat with him, she wanted to talk to him. It was just so easy. So right.

Damn it, what was she doing?

"So, what do you say?"

Shutting off her brain, she nodded, "Six?"

A slow grin moved across his lips. "Yeah."

She nodded. "Sounds good to me."

It did, but that didn't mean it was a good thing.

CHAPTER 14

"I'm crazy."

Delaney laughed on the other end of the line as Gen moved her hands down the front of her dress, inhaled hard, and shook her head. This wasn't the smartest idea, but when was she ever smart when it came to Theo Hudson? "I think it's just right."

"Del, he is still in love with me."

"I know."

Gen gasped. "What?"

"Everyone knows, Gen. He's loved you as long as he's known you. He's one of those lucky folks who got the whole love at first sight bit. I'm jealous, and you know darn well I'm Team Theo."

Gen couldn't fathom it. Yes, she'd been attracted to him immediately, and yes, she fell in love days later, but not at first sight. No, that wasn't even real. Except in books, of course. Filling her cheeks with breath, she blew out as she shook her head at her appearance. She was cute in the floral printed dress, her hair up in a large bun and her makeup done soft, but she looked nervous.

"I feel like I can't start something with Theo right now. I'm not ready."

"Tell him that."

"Like he'd listen," she commented, looking out the window where he had a table and chairs set up on the dock. He was lighting a candle, and even from her window, she knew he looked gorgeous. He was wearing a soft yellow button-down, some of those old jeans, and his boots. Her heart raced, and she was shocked to realize she still loved him too. "I can't believe it, but I still love him."

"Of course you do." Delaney laughed. "You two are made for each other."

"I'm just not ready. It wouldn't be fair to him, or me, for me just to jump back in after five long years with someone else."

"Again, Gen, tell him that. He's a great listener, and he'll do just about anything for you."

"I haven't even told him I called it off with Montgomery."

"Yeah, do that."

Gen rolled her eyes. "You're not helping here."

"Team Theo!"

"Loser, I'll talk to you later."

Delaney giggled as she said, "Wait, don't hang up."

"What?"

"Randy's house, you want me to tell them you want it?" Gen bit her lip. She had been thinking about it all day since she got the text from Delaney that someone else was looking at the house. "I think you do."

Gen wasn't sure how she'd do it. Would she go home and get her things, bring them down to Spring Grove? Or have them delivered? She wasn't sure, but she really needed to face Montgomery first. No matter what, she knew she would be coming back. She couldn't leave again. Not for good, at least. This place was her home.

And Theo was there.

"I'm a mess."

"Yup, so that's a yes?"

Exhaling heavily, she nodded even though Delaney couldn't see her. "Yes."

"Yee-haw! Okay, I'll get back with you tomorrow. Good luck! Use protection unless you're ready for a kid. Then free the beast, girl. Get it!"

And then the line went dead.

Rolling her eyes, Gen threw her phone down and headed downstairs. When she reached the kitchen, Theo was coming in from the patio. His gaze fell on her, and his lips slowly curved. "Mercy me, Genny. Trying to kill me tonight?"

She waved him off. "It's just a dress."

"One that was made to be my undoing," he announced, holding his hand out. She was hesitant and completely breathless, but she took his hand as he intertwined their fingers. "Let's go." After reaching for a bottle of wine, he led them out into the summer night. "I made some fried chicken and greens."

"Yum."

"Figured you'd love that."

"You figured right."

She inhaled softly, and when she looked up at him, he was watching her. Again. She'd never felt so beautiful in someone else's eyes. Not even when Montgomery would look at her did she know what he was thinking. But with Theo, his eyes said it all. He wanted her. Soon, they were both smiling, which caused her to look away so her heart wouldn't come out of her chest and land on the grass for him to see.

As they reached the table, he held her chair out for her. She sat down and sent him a smile. He sat across from her and poured them each a glass of wine. "You still drink, right?" he asked, filling her cup to the top.

She giggled. "I do. Just out of a glass now."

"Ah, classy lady," he teased, and he smiled as he filled his just the same. Reaching across the table, he took her hands, and she was confused until he bowed his head, saying grace over their food.

"And thank you, Lord, for bringing her back. Amen."

Gen looked up, their gazes meeting, and repeated, "Amen." Her grin grew as she opened her napkin, laying it on her lap. "So."

"So." He dug in, taking one of the chicken legs before stuffing it in his mouth, getting most of the meat off the bone. A silence fell between them as she picked at her mac and cheese. When she looked up at him, he was sucking the bone, his eyes on her. "Am I making you uncomfortable?"

She scoffed. "Not at all."

"Your brows are touching, so you're uncomfortable or confused. Which is it?"

She gave him a look as she relaxed her face. "Neither, thank you."

"Sure."

She rolled her eyes as she took a bite of the mac and cheese. It was magnificent. Groaning as it went down her throat, she pointed her fork at him. "Perfection."

"Thank you, ma'am." He tipped his imaginary hat to her before digging back in.

Taking a sip of her wine, she held the glass in her hands as she enjoyed the peacefulness of the lake. "It's so beautiful."

"You are."

She gave him a sideways glance and sighed. "You're ruthless."

"That I am."

Turning to look at him, she smiled. "So tell me everything."

"Everything?"

"Yes, last ten years, what you did, who you did it with, everything."

He eyed her. "You first."

She eyed him back, but he just shot her that devilish grin of his that made her heart go wild in her chest and her body break out in gooseflesh. "Fine. I stayed here about two weeks after you went to jail."

"Two weeks? Why?"

"I was hoping you'd get out."

"What did you do for money?"

"I used my dad's credit card."

"The emergency card? Naughty girl."

She chuckled ruefully. "That's how he found me."

"Oh. Well, that sucks."

"Yeah, he made me leave. I went to college."

"How many men fell under your spell?"

She rolled her eyes. "I didn't date anyone."

"Really?"

"Yeah, I just slept around."

"Sounds about right," he teased, and she grinned over at him.

"You make me sound like a whore."

"Nah, just a girl with a plan."

"I always have a plan."

"Yeah, you do."

She gave him a sneaky grin and then let out a long breath before grabbing her glass once more, taking a sip. "I graduated, wrote my first novel, shopped it around, and got signed. It was awesome. Especially when I hit the *New York Times*, that was one of best moments of my life. I was actually out celebrating when I met back up with Montgomery."

"And he stole your heart?"

She shrugged. "No, but he was fun to sleep with, and then he somehow talked me into dating him. And then—"

"The rest is history."

"Yeah."

A silence fell between them as he devoured the rest of his chicken. She watched as his brow furrowed and his jaw ticked. He was annoyed. When he looked up, cleaning his teeth with his tongue, he made a clicking noise before he asked, "Fun to sleep with, huh?"

She laughed at that. "Of course that's the part that hangs you up."

"Yes, because I thought I was fun to sleep with. You loved it."

"I did. But I don't know if you remember, but you got thrown in jail, and I never saw you again."

"Yeah, I do remember that."

"I was holding out for ya. I came here all the time until the moment he proposed. Then I stopped."

"Why?"

"He didn't want me here."

"Hmm."

She nodded, hating how stupid she sounded. Montgomery didn't want her there. Who the hell cared? This was her spot, her second home, but then, she had to respect him, didn't she? Well, if that was the case, why hadn't she respected him when he asked her not to come this time? Shaking her head, she said, "So now you."

He looked up, wiping his mouth as he nodded. "I went to jail. Two long years. I wrote to you every day."

Her lips curved. "You did? Why didn't you send them?"

"I didn't know your address, and the letters were dumb. I just told ya I loved you in a billion different ways," he said, chuckling as he looked out at the lake. "I'd think of ya every night. The way your hair flew in the wind when we were driving here. The way your face burned so quickly that one day. Your laugh, your touch... Your kisses about did me in when I was stuck in that cell."

She ran her tongue along her lips. "You should have sent the letters. I would have loved them."

"I know, but what was the point? I was a convicted felon," he laughed. "God, I was stupid."

"Just a bit."

He flashed her a grin. "But I got out. Begged Old Man McElroy to give me a job, he did, and I worked for five long years up at the distillery. I always helped everyone out, stuff around the diner, Mawmaw Pearl still has me mowing her lawn whenever Holden can't come do it for her, which is a lot since he's so damn busy up at the distillery. But I did a lot of side work for Ms. Neil here at the Blu. I loved the place before I started working here, but when she had me crawling all over hell and high water in this place, I just fell harder. Or maybe it was the memories of this place, our memories that had me coming back all the time."

She was breathless, watching as he talked. Clearing her throat, she whispered, "We had some damn good memories."

He nodded, a grin curving his lips. "I think I did you on this dock."

She snickered. "And in the lake."

He laughed, his head falling back as he shook his head. "Man, we were wild."

"Sure were."

His gaze met back up with hers, and he nodded. "And when Ms. Neil passed, I had so much money saved up since I didn't have anywhere, or anyone, for that matter, to spend it—"

"Please, all the girls would want you around here."

"Oh, they wanted, and I gave some to some, but no one got my heart. No one. Except you." She looked away, a smile fighting the urge to spread. He had a way of making her feel so damn good. "But I bought the place, and for the last four years, I've turned a damn good profit. It's doing wonderful. I mean, I'm no Zoe Jayne."

She rolled her eyes. "Some would think you're better."

He scoffed. "Please."

"I think so." Once the words left her mouth, he inhaled deeply as he leaned on the table, taking one of her hands in his and lacing their fingers together. Her breath caught at the simple touch, and when his eyes met hers, chills ran down her spine.

"I did it for you, Genny. All of it. You know that, right?"

She slowly nodded. "I suspect so."

"I did it for us."

"Theo."

"No, listen—"

But before he could continue, a truck screeched to a stop on the side of the Blu, and Holden jumped out in a hurry. "Asshole, where is your phone?"

Theo stood, and Gen did the same. "In the house. We're having dinner."

"That's fine and dandy, but I've been calling you, Pearl's callin', hell, even Jackie called."

Theo was moving up the dock, and Gen rushed to catch up. "Why, what the hell's wrong?"

"Delaney found out Larry's been cheating."

Theo paused, causing Gen to run smack into the middle of his back with a umph. "Shit. What?"

"Yup, with Annalee."

"What?"

"Yup," Holden said slowly, shaking his head. "And Delaney's got her Louisville."

Gen had no clue what was happening, or what that even meant, but by the looks on Holden's and Theo's faces, it didn't mean anything good.

CHAPTER 15

W hen Theo pulled into the spot next to Holden, Gen's eyes widened at the sight of Delaney on the top of a very nice black Mustang.

Swinging the bat into the hood.

"Del, get down. Please stop. Oh, fuck," Larry yelled as he ducked when she swung it at him.

"How dare you! With Annalee! The town slut! Are you fucking kidding me? I am a joy, a fucking delight, and I am gorgeous! You were lucky I was fucking you!"

"Tell him, Del," someone in the crowd yelled as she slammed the bat into the windshield, people gasping and grimacing at the damage that was done. When Larry screamed, running to the only police officer in Spring Grove, Gen's eyes almost fell out of her head.

He was eating a donut and drinking some coffee.

"Bryce, do something!"

Bryce, who Gen thought was Old Man McElroy's youngest son, just shrugged. "Sorry, this donut and coffee are damn good. Have you tried them yet?"

"This isn't fair! She gets away with murder in this town! Why, 'cause she plays on your softball team?"

"I don't see anything," he said simply.

"You fucking ginger ass—" Larry started, but when Bryce stood to his full height, Larry's words fell off abruptly.

"I'm sorry, what?"

Larry just let out a yell as he ran back to where Delaney was not holding back at all. "Del, stop! This is madness! We weren't in love."

She whipped around, swinging the bat at him once more. "But we could have been! Now I'm going to have to go back to online dating, you son of a fat bitch!"

Larry gasped. "My momma ain't fat!"

"No, she is not. She is a very nice woman, but she raised a shit-for-brains asshole!"

"Damn, she's mad," Gen observed, and both Holden and Theo nodded.

"Theo, please do something," Pearl said as she came up. "She swung the bat at Holden."

Theo exhaled harshly as he shook his head, squeezing Gen's hand. "Give me a moment, all right?"

"Of course," Gen said as he headed toward where Delaney was knocking off the side mirrors with a grunt at each one. "I've never seen her this mad."

"She doesn't do cheating, that's for sure," Holden said with a shake of his head. "Hey, you know Theo is still digging you, right?"

Gen smiled. "I know. Thanks, Holden."

He just nodded, sending her a grin as she brought her attention to where Theo was calmly talking to Delaney, who was paying him no mind. "Del, come on. Let's get down before you get hurt."

"No, Theo! He cheated on me! I hate him."

"I am aware, and you have every right to lose your ever-loving shit, but we need to stop. Bryce is gonna be done with that donut soon."

Delaney paused, looking back at Bryce, who waved, and then

to Theo. "Go buy him a fucking 'nother one!" Theo grimaced as she started on the top of the car. "It isn't fair! I'll never be able to find someone to love me the way you love Gen. Or hell, the way anyone loves anyone in this fucking town! I'm always stuck with the motherfucking bag of herpes dicks!"

When she swung hard once more, the bat hit the frame of the car, shattering into pieces. She screamed, and Gen's heart broke for her. Tears were streaming down her beautiful, flushed face, and she just looked broken. When Delaney fell onto the car, sitting with a huff, Gen found tears gathering in her own eyes.

"All right, show's over," Bryce said finally, coming off his car, wiping his hands. Coming toward Delaney, he tapped her knee. "You're done, Del."

"I'm done," she cried as Theo gathered her up, holding her close as she cried. Gen watched for a moment and knew she would never meet anyone else like him. She'd never encounter a town like this, where everyone looked after everyone. She loved this place, and boy, did she love that man. But before she could even move, go and join them, she could see that behind them stood the last person she ever thought she'd see in Spring Grove.

Montgomery.

Surely, she was seeing things, but she really wasn't. He was standing there, a wide-eyed expression on his face. When his gaze met Gen's, he shook his head and then pointed to where there wasn't a crowd. Gen drew her brows together as she made her way to him around the crowd so that no one would notice.

"Does that happen all the time? That's crazy."

Gen shook her head. "No, not at all." With wide eyes herself, she asked, "What are you doing here?"

"Well, hello to you too," he answered, his movements very stiff. It was obvious he didn't want to be there.

"Oh, I'm sorry, it's been radio silence from you, and then you just pop up?"

He shrugged. "I wanted to come talk to you."

Her heart started to jackhammer in her chest. "What for? You've said enough, I think."

"I don't like the way you ended things."

"Did you give me much of a choice? I mean, fuck, Mont, you accused me of shit, left and right."

"'Cause I knew it was over. When you left, I knew you were leaving me."

"That wasn't my intention at first."

He shook his head. "And now?"

She didn't even hesitate. "We're done." He looked away, his beautiful face pained as he seemed not to understand her words. "I won't be with someone who doesn't support me, who accuses me of stuff I wasn't doing—"

"Fine, I'll support you. Write your heart out, just don't end this."

She shook her head. "Mont, it doesn't work like that. The damage is done."

He scoffed. "Is it? Or is it because that bastard is watching us?"

Her eyes burned into Montgomery's. She didn't have to look to know that Theo was watching. She fully expected him to. Hell, she expected a damn circle to form soon. That was Spring Grove, nothing was ever private, but she wouldn't let Montgomery think that. "I was done on day three of being here when you wouldn't answer my calls."

"I am a busy man."

"You're right. Way too busy for me."

He sighed, shaking his head. "I want to be with you. Gen, don't you understand that?"

She eyed him, not the least bit convinced. Something was off. "Your mom make you come here?"

He grimaced, shaking his head. "No. I wanted to."

"Okay, then why haven't you told me you love me?"

He looked up at her. "That's understood—"

"No," she said, shaking her head. "No, it's not."

He seemed put off as he threw his hands up. "Fine, I love you."

When laughter came from beside them, she finally looked to see Theo approaching. "Damn, thank God I never learned how to tell a woman I loved her from my big bro."

"Theo, stop," she warned, but he wasn't listening. His gaze was on Montgomery's.

"You don't love her. You probably never did."

"You don't know shit, you piece of shit."

Theo shrugged. "I don't know, I feel you may be the POS, friend."

"I'm not your friend," Mont sneered, his eyes fiery as he shook his head. "You think she's yours? No, she's mine."

"Ha, she was never yours. She was always mine."

"Really? Who's been fucking her for the last five years?"

"That's all you've done. You haven't loved her," Theo said, not the least bit affected by his words. "If you loved her, you wouldn't be speaking like that about her."

"You don't know shit."

"I know a lot, friend, and I know she doesn't love you."

Montgomery's face went red. "Get the hell out of here."

Theo was untroubled as he looked back at Gen. "I'm good."

Montgomery was shaking with anger as he glared. "I'd like to talk to my fiancée."

Theo went to say something, but Gen stopped him. "I'm not your fiancée, Montgomery. That's over."

Theo's head whipped to her as Montgomery said, "We don't need to end this."

"Yes, we do." She could feel Theo burning a hole in the side of her head with his gaze, but she held Montgomery's. "You hurt me. I won't be with someone who doesn't believe in me. Trust me. Or above all, really love me. We've been comfortable. It's been easy between us for whatever reason, maybe just ignoring the things we don't like about each other, but I refuse to live like that. I want to be in love with someone who sets my soul on fire, and I'm sorry, you don't do that, Montgomery."

Montgomery held her gaze, his eyes flashing with anger as he sneered, "But this guy does all that? I knew you weren't over him—"

"He has nothing to do with this. I made this decision before I saw him."

"So, that's it?"

She nodded. "That's it."

"Did you even love me?"

Gen's eyes filled with tears. "I think so. Did you?"

Looking away once more, Montgomery swallowed hard. "I did."

"Then I'm sorry."

"Yeah, me too."

"So you broke it off with him?" Theo asked, and she turned, nodding her head.

"I did. I was gonna tell you today."

A grin pulled at Theo's mouth as he took a step toward her. "You should have told me sooner so I could have done this." And before she knew it, he held her face in his hands as he gave her the kind of kiss that would make a porn star blush. Holding on to his wrists, she didn't fight it. She wanted it. She knew it was awful and rude to do in front of Montgomery, but she couldn't help it. She was a victim of pure lust when it came to Theo. When they parted, their noses knocking, her soul sang for him as he grinned down at her.

Pulling away, she went to apologize to Montgomery, but he was already walking away, and her heart sank. "You shouldn't have done that in front of him."

"Why?" Theo asked, holding her hips in his hands. "He had to know that you've been mine all this time."

"Theo," she said, looking up at him. "I did care for him. I may have even loved him at one time."

He didn't like that, but he shrugged just the same, holding her gaze. "In the past. Now, we have the future. Now, listen—"

But Gen shook her head. "No, I need to say something."

"Let me get this out first," he asked, a playful grin on his face.

"Genevieve, I've loved you my whole adult life, and I never want to stop. I know we've had some time apart, I know we aren't the same damn people we were then, but surely you feel what I feel. That undeniable pull between us. We're meant for each other, darling, you and me. And I know you just came out of a relationship, but I need you. Just you. While, for a long time, I didn't think I was good enough for you, and I still may not be, I want to try, Genny. I've learned a lot about life since the moment we were ripped apart, and I'm ready. I love you. Mercy me, I love you so damn much, I can't stand it."

She swallowed past the sob in her throat as she gazed up into his beautiful face. The face she had loved for as long as she could remember, the same face she'd missed more than her next breath. He was standing there. Ready.

But she wasn't.

"I'm sorry—"

"No," he moaned. "You don't love me? Really, Genny?"

She held up her hand. "Can I finish?" He eyed her, taking a deep breath as he nodded. "Theo, I'm sorry, but I'm just not ready to jump back into something when I don't even have my life together. I have to get my stuff, bring it here, and I just... I need time. I need time to figure out me, to fix whatever comes up, and to lick my wounds a bit. I mean, I was with him five years. That's a long time."

Letting her go, he looked away as he swallowed. "Can we not do all that together? I can help."

"No, because if I come to you, I want to be whole. I want to be ready to be all in like you are right now."

Moving his hand down his face, he smacked his lips as he nodded in understanding. "All right. What can I help with?"

She shook her head. "I have to do it myself."

He cleared his throat, and she could see the tears in his eyes. Silence fell between them, and she could feel the people watching them. They weren't close, but they sure did want to know what was happening. When Theo looked back at her, he swallowed hard. "I can help move things, just call me. You have my number. It's the Blu's number."

"Okay."

"And you can stay as long as you need, until you get to wherever you're going. Or if you want to stay with me, you're welcome."

She reached out, taking his hand in hers. "I'm gonna rent Randy's old place."

He nodded. "All right, then." She squeezed his hand, and he looked down at her. "This blows."

She smiled. "It's for the best."

"Because I do love you, Genevieve. I do."

"And I love you, Theo," she whispered. "But I don't like who I am at this moment in time."

He looked away once more. "When will you?"

She shrugged. "A year? I don't know."

Inhaling hard, he let it out slowly and nodded. "I'll be there."

"There?"

"In a year, with a ring."

"Theo," she said, shaking her head.

But he didn't answer. Instead, he took her mouth with his and kissed her long and hard. She drank from him in the most succulent way that had her toes curling in her flip-flops. When he pulled away, he kissed her nose and then the side of her mouth. "I'll see you around, and if you need anything, you know my number."

"I do."

"Are you good getting home? I'm going to the bar. I got a date with a bottle of McElroy."

She smiled as she nodded. "I'm fine. I'm gonna go for a walk."

"Cool, I'll see ya."

"See ya."

He kissed her nose one last time and then walked away. As Gen watched him, she almost called him back, she did. They'd had so much time apart that she didn't want any more, but she knew this was for the best.

Not only for him, but for her too.

EPILOGUE

"So, what are you working on?"

Gen looked over to where Delaney was lying across her couch, playing with her hair. When Gen had moved in to Randy's little cabin, it was already adorable, but it was still him, it wasn't Gen. Now, it was Gen. The room was bright, no curtains, and beautiful light blue paint on the walls. She had no furniture from when she moved out of Montgomery's; he had kept everything with good reason. So when she went shopping, she knew she wouldn't need much since the cabin was so small. But it was perfect for her and even had enough room for when her parents came to stay, which had been a lot in the last year. They loved Spring Grove as much as she did.

Glancing back at her best friend, she smiled. "I'm finishing up Travis and Ashley's novella."

"Which means?"

"Basically, about their lives two years later."

"Oh, are they married?"

Gen beamed. "Yes, with beautiful babies and lots of great butt sex, things are good for Travis and Ashley."

"Yeah, they're getting more action than we are," Delaney said sadly. "I'm jealous of fictional characters. That's pathetic."

Gen giggled as she wrote The End before closing her laptop. "Sometimes I'm jealous of them too."

"Why? All you have to do is snap your fingers, and Theo would drop diamonds all over you while doing you. I hate you."

Gen rolled her eyes. "He would not."

"He's here all the time, helping you with things."

"Because he's a good guy."

"He's still head over heels for you, and if you got your head out of your ass, you'd notice that this year meant nothing but time for y'all to hang out."

Gen looked away, drawing in a deep breath. She wanted to say it had been easy being around Theo and not kissing him or touching him, but it hadn't. Though they got along perfectly and enjoyed hanging with their friends, she missed him. He was respecting her space, and she appreciated it. She needed that because with each passing day, she was slowly finding herself, finding who she was. She realized a lot of that had to do with the town. She loved it, she loved the people, but most of all, she still loved Theo. So damn much. But the problem was, now she was worried she didn't deserve him.

"I don't know. I let him down pretty rough."

"So? He's been through worse—hello, jail—and he made it through that because he knew one day you'd come back to him."

Gen eyed Delaney. "Are you his spokesgirl?"

"Damn right," she said with a wink. "You know I'm Team Theo."

"I'm aware."

"And you can't deny he's as hot as the summer is long," she said, tipping her chin toward Gen. She wasn't sure what Delaney was doing until she heard movement behind her. When Gen turned in her seat, Theo was out front with the tools to finish the patio. He was replacing the bricks because Gen had fallen and broken her ankle a couple of days ago. He was absolutely nothing like his brother. Unlike Theo, who she knew hadn't dated this whole year, Montgomery had married his assistant...six months after Gen had called it off. She had to assume he had been cheating, but she knew, either way, the truth would drive her insane. So instead, she drowned herself in work and wrote three books that year.

That was, when she wasn't distracted by Theo.

Which was a lot since she found he was always wherever she was.

With the same fluttery feeling that had met her every single time she saw him, she breathed, "He's here early."

Delaney just smiled. "Because he knows you're here."

"Del."

"Gen." She shot her a sneaky grin and then shook her head. "He's always here, just waiting."

"I know," she said as an exhale.

"I know you're lonely. Especially in this little cabin all by yourself."

"I am," she admitted, watching until he looked up, waving. She waved back as Delaney came up beside her.

"And you're ready."

"I am?"

"Oh yeah, I know you are," Delaney said before kissing the top of Gen's head. "I'm gonna get out of here. Mawmaw needs help with some honeybee thing, I don't know. Call me if you sleep with him."

"Why would I do that?"

"So I can live vicariously through you."

Gen rolled her eyes as she laughed. "See ya."

"Bye, girl."

When the door shut, Gen turned in her seat to watch as Theo knocked the old bricks out. Standing, she winced as she limped to the door, pushing it open. "You're early."

"Hey, you're supposed to be off that ankle."

"It's been almost a week. I'm fine."

"You aren't," he said, coming toward her so that she would sit back down. "If you want to bother me, I'll come in here and get a beer. You've got beer, right?"

She wrinkled her nose at him as he cut to her fridge, grabbing a beer. He held one out to her, but she shook her head. "That's how I fell."

"Can't handle your beer?" he teased, and she laughed.

"McElroy's whiskey."

"Yeah, why are you still playing with that stuff?"

She shrugged. "Sometimes, I think I can handle it."

He sat down across from her. "You can't."

She nodded as she held out her ankle. "I can't."

Taking her ankle softly, he laid it over his leg, and tingles ran up her legs from his mere touch. "Aren't you supposed to keep this thing elevated? Damn, this cast is heavy."

"It is," she laughed, and he smiled over at her. "How was your day?"

"Long," he said before taking a pull of his beer. "If I didn't have enough going on at the Blu, I had Holden needing help up at the distillery."

"You working for free?"

He shot her a dry look. "No, I get a cut of Holden's pay."

"Nice."

"Yeah, but I'm whupped."

"Go on home. The patio can wait."

"Nah, I'm good," he said, letting out a long breath. "What did you do today? Finish Travis and Ashley? Everyone live happily ever? Matt good?"

She smiled. "They are. Lots of butt sex too."

"Good, Travis likes it."

Gen giggled. "He does."

He exhaled and then looked over at her. "You look good today."

"Hush, I'm a mess, and shit, Delaney forgot to help me with my shower. Ugh, I'll have to wait till tomorrow. Something about honeybees." When Theo waggled his brows, she rolled her eyes. "I haven't shaved anything in over a week, you aren't seeing me naked."

"I like rugged. See my beard."

"You're crazy. Hush."

He laughed as he moved his hand down her shin to her knee, rubbing it gently as her eyes drifted shut. Soon a stillness fell between them. The sounds of the lake filled the room since the patio door was open. A group of kids was having a blast, and Gen wanted so badly to go out there. But at the same time, she was in great company. "Hey."

She opened her eyes. "Hey."

"You have a date for the Fourth thing?"

Her brows pulled together. "You asking to be my help that night?"

He scoffed. "Actually, I wanted to be your date."

"Which means you'll be my helper since I don't walk well."

"Are you saying yes?"

"I am," she teased, and he beamed back at her. His eyes were playful, but there was a bit of lust swirling deep in those blue depths. She wasn't sure why, but she said, "I'm surprised you're asking."

"Are ya?"

"I am."

"Why?"

"Well, I mean, I didn't think you'd want to. I don't know."

"Why wouldn't I want to?"

"I don't know," she laughed, waving him off. "I just thought—"

"Well, it's been a year."

"It has."

"And you know I said in a year I'd be here—with a ring."

Her head fell to the side. "You did say that."

"And it's been exactly a year since you broke my heart in the middle of the square."

"I didn't break your—" She went to protest, but she was stunned to silence when he leaned to the left and dug into his pocket. When he set a box on the table, her eyes widened. "Really?"

He was smiling before his gaze met hers. "A year ago, I told you I'd love you until my dying day. I wasn't lying, Gen. I love you. I loved you then, I loved you in between, and I'll love you for the rest of my days. This stupid long year that you've put me through only made me love you more."

"Theo—"

"You needed help moving in, I was here. I made sure to know exactly where you were gonna be, just so I could be there too. All those dinners where I invited everyone, it was so I knew you'd come. Just so I could see you. Be with you. I've been patient, I've respected your space because I wanted you to be ready for me. Genny, fuck, I love you. So fucking much."

Emotion clogged her throat as she watched him struggle, though a grin stayed on his lips. "I'll never ever love anyone like you, nor do I want to. I know we haven't dated—hell, I don't even think that dinner on the lake could be called a date. But in a way, I don't want to date you, I want to live my life with you. I want to be yours. Only yours. And for that to happen, I need you to take this ring, put it on, and say yes to being my other half. Being right where you belong." Gen was pretty sure her heart had just stopped dead in her chest as he gazed deep into her eyes. "You could say no, and that still wouldn't derail me from coming back in another year and trying again because, darling, you're it. You're my darling, my everything. Say yes to me."

Leaning on the table, she reached for the box, opening it to see a sweet little ring, a diamond that didn't even come close to what Montgomery had given her way back when. But what Montgomery's ring didn't have that Theo's did was the promise that he would love her for the rest of his days just like he said. And Theo would always make sure she knew that. She'd never question him. Never have to wonder because he'd tell her.

She looked up, and a grin pulled at her lips as she slowly slid the ring on before reaching across the table and taking his hand in hers.

"You told me a long time ago that you weren't the one for me."

He nodded. "I was wrong. I was an idiot because you're it."

"Yeah, you were." She swallowed hard, moving her thumb along the back of his hand as she held his gaze. "I thought you didn't want me anymore."

He laughed. "I'll always want you, darling. Always." A grin pulled at his lips as she held his gaze. "Say it. Mercy, Gen, say it."

She kissed the back of his hand, and with her lips still in place, she whispered the only word he wanted.

"Yes."

THE END

You know you don't want to miss what is coming next! Click here to signup for my newsletter, and never miss another announcement about upcoming works, new releases, exclusive excerpts and giveaways! I do an awesome monthly gift box that I know you'll love! So join now!

KEEP READING FOR A PREVIEW OF WHISKEY PRINCE!

EXCERPT OF WHISKEY PRINCE

AMBERLYN

I'm an orphan.

When I lost my father, I remember feeling like I would never breathe again. I was Daddy's little girl. He made me feel like a princess, he loved me the way a father should, and he spoiled me in every way possible. He was a very handsome man, with dark brown hair, light green eyes, and dark stubble that he left a little longer than he should because it gave my mother a reason to fuss at him. He loved when she fussed at him; he said it meant she loved him. He had a low, tenor voice, one that could be used to do the commentary for movies or documentaries. He used to sing to me, an old song from his homeland. Even now, when I am nervous, I sing it. It helps. Somehow, it helps dull the pain of not having him.

I was twelve when we lost him to a drunk driver.

Somehow, my mother and I survived losing him, though. We learned to go on with him still deep in our hearts and souls. We helped each other to cope with the pain of losing him. She was not only the most amazing mother, but she was a great father too.

Some days were hard. I'd wake up and say I was having a bad Dad day, and she would reply that she was, too. We would just cry, for hours, but then she would hug me tightly, tell me that the sun was shining and so shall we, and we did until the day she found out she had throat cancer.

My favorite thing about my mother was her smile, but she soon stopped smiling and so did I. The day I found her at the table with tears dripping from her eyes, I asked if she was having a bad Dad day, and she shook her head and just kept apologizing. I didn't understand, and when she told me what was going on, I didn't want to believe it. It couldn't be happening. I had already lost my dad and now my mom, too? It wasn't fair.

When you were eighteen, you were supposed to be excited for prom, boyfriends, going off to college, and starting a new, refreshing life. But not me. All that came to a halting stop. My dreams of learning the written word, and maybe meeting a boy to spend time with, went up in flames. Instead, I became a caregiver for my mother. I stayed home and studied online as I waited hand and foot on her. I watched for two years as my mother slowly died before my eyes, and to be honest, I don't think I'd have it any other way. At least I know she went, knowing I loved her more than life itself, when she cupped my face and slowly took her last breath before joining my father in heaven.

When the hospice nurses came after I tucked my mother in bed and had a good, long cry, they were surprised how strong I was and commended me on it. I said it was because of her, and how she raised me to be strong. They knew she begged me to put her in a home, but I'd be damned. She was my best friend. She cared for me my whole life, and I was going to care for her. Plus, I knew she felt more comfortable with me than some nurses she didn't know. It wasn't as if her parents could come and help. They had long passed before I was even born. All she had was her brother who lived in New York, and he couldn't be bothered with her.

Even now, as I watch him from across my mother's casket, which is covered in beautiful, white roses, I can't help but wonder why he came. He isn't even crying. He is just standing there, with the same blue eyes as my mother, looking as if he'd rather be playing golf than acting as if he is mourning her. I choke back the tears as I look around at all the people who have come to pay their respects—neighbors, family friends, and coworkers. Even some of my old high school teachers are here, and I feel nothing. I want to jump into that casket with her and go to heaven too. I don't want or know how to go on without her. Who is going to help me mourn her?

Wiping away the tears rolling down my cheeks, I take in a deep breath as I softly start to sing my father's song. In my head, I hear only my parents and not myself as they softly sing Liam Clancy's, "The Parting Glass" to me. My mother couldn't sing for anything, but none of us cared. We would all sing, and most of all, we were all happy. But now, my throat feels tight, my limbs are numb, and I just feel empty.

When the song I am singing plays over the speakers, that's when I squeeze my eyes tight because I know they are lowering her into the ground. I don't want to see it. I hate knowing it is happening. Soon, it is over and everyone is hugging me, gently squeezing my hands, wishing me well, and saying that they are there for me if I need them. When my uncle is the last to come up to me, I want to scream at him, *Why did you come?* I hate that he wasn't there for her because I know if I had a sibling, I would always be there for them. Especially someone like my mom—she was so sweet, so caring, so loving—and he couldn't even be there at the end for her. Couldn't be there for me. His only niece.

I can tell he is uncomfortable, and I'm glad he is. As he runs his hands through his dark red hair, he lets out a breath before saying, "Amberlyn, I'm sorry for your loss."

"It's your loss, too," I say, crossing my arms over my chest. The dress I'm wearing scratches my ribs, and I want to pull at it, but I don't. Instead, I hold his gaze as he slowly nods.

"You're right, our loss, and I want you to know that I am here if you need anything."

"I won't."

He looks away. "Yeah, I know you won't, but in case you do."

I don't say anything, even knowing he is waiting for me to. What does he want me to say? Thank you? Hell no.

"Anyway, here," he says, opening his suit jacket to pull out an envelope. "Ciara wanted me to give this to you."

I take it quickly because I see my name in my mom's hand-writing on the front. "What is it?"

"I don't know," he answers. "She sent it to me in a letter and said to give it to you on the day of her funeral. She also told me to tell you to call me once you've read it, and I'll tell you what we will do next."

I'm confused. I look up with my brows pulled together as I say, "What? Do what next? I am going to pick up the pieces and figure out how to live without her. How the hell are you going to help me with that?"

He runs his hands through his unruly hair, and I see something I haven't seen all day—pain. He is in pain, and it completely boggles my mind. He didn't care about her or me—why is he in pain?

"Just read the letter, Amberlyn. When you are done, call me, and we will go from there. Again, I'm sorry and I wish that things had played out differently. I cared more about work than I did my family, and now I have to live with that for the rest of my life."

With that, he turns and starts to walk away. I watch his retreating back and without thinking, I say, "Yeah, you did."

I follow behind him to where my beat-up, red Honda is waiting for me. Jumping into it, I numbly drive home to the house I grew up in. A beautiful, ranch-style home is one of six that surround a large lake. There is a dock out back that I would sit on for hours and read until my eyes hurt. There wasn't a summer day that my mom or dad didn't find me out there almost sunburned, claiming I only needed to read one more chapter.

I love this house and I love this neighborhood, but I just don't know if I can live here anymore. The thought of leaving has my stomach in knots though. I know there is money coming in, and I could sell the house and start over, but where? How? How am I supposed to live without her? Without him?

Shaking my head before I start to sob, I push my key into the lock, unlock the door, and then enter the house. Parts of my mother and father are everywhere, along with parts of me. My dad's guitars still sit in the corner, untouched for the last eight years. My mother's knitting things are still overflowing in a basket by her favorite chair, along with all her law books, which I used to read to her to calm her at night when the pain was unbearable. And then everywhere I look is a notebook or a novel of my own. The house looks exactly the same, and I feel it shouldn't. I feel that it should look different or changed, the way I feel I have.

Forcing my feet to move, I head to my mother's room, ignoring her hospital bed, and falling into the one she shared with my father. Taking in a deep breath, her flowery scent intoxicates me. I close my eyes to imagine her beside me, her eyes a bright blue, not the dull color they were before she passed, and her bright red hair falling in heaps of curls around her face as she softly ran her slender fingers through my dark, brownish red hair.

When tears start leaking from my closed eyes, I take in a shuddering breath before I open them and stare up at the ceiling. Her letter is burning in my fingers, and a part of me doesn't even want to read it right now. I want to ignore it all—act like the last couple days didn't happen, but I know I can't. Not only is my uncle expecting my call, but I am also curious why.

So I open the letter. When a check for ten thousand dollars and what looks like a plane ticket falls onto my chest, I ignore them. Through tear-filled eyes, I read my mother's letter.

MY DEAR, SWEET AMBERLYN,

I'm so terribly sorry. I don't think I can apologize enough for not being there for you as you start your adult life. I hate that your life has been so hard, and I wish that there were a way I could change it all, but I can't. I feel though, that instead of letting this hold you back, you should grow. I believe I have given you all the tools to make your life the best it can be. You are smart, beautiful, and unbelievably talented. And more than anything, I want you to live your dreams.

I know you are probably lying in my bed, wrapped up in a little ball, and bawling your eyes out. Baby, that is fine. Cry. Cry it all out. Then remember that the sun is shining, and you have to as well. As much as I wish I were there with my arms around you, I can't be, but I am in your heart, along with your father, and baby, we love you. So much.

I know that your uncle Felix said for you to call him after reading this, and you are probably wondering why, so let me explain. I don't want you to live in the past, and I have a feeling you will. I think that you won't have a reason to get out of bed if you stay in the home that we built. You've never really made friends, never really dated, and I want you to do those things, but will you if you are living in our home? I don't think so. So here is what I propose: Your father's sister has offered to take you in at her bed and breakfast. Back home, in Ireland.

I think our biggest mistake was moving to the States, but your father was convinced that he was going to be a singer. I believed in him, so we left. As you know, it didn't work out, but we made a life here and never went back. I wish we had, and I'm sorry we didn't, but now you have the chance. This is the opportunity of a lifetime for you. Something I know your father would have wanted you to do.

So go for a year, work for your aunt, go to school, and live, my sweetheart. There is so much history in Ireland, and I think you'll not only enjoy the beautiful world but the people as well. I know this seems drastic and that I am asking a lot of you, but my sweet darling, I am worried you'll get stuck, and I don't want that for you. I want you to live all your dreams, and I think Ireland is the best place to do that.

So go. Your aunt, Shelia, is expecting a call to let her know you are coming. She also holds the next letter that I have written for you so, if anything, you should go for that. It has my wishes for you. After a year, if you haven't made Ireland your home, then come back and everything will be here for you. Uncle Felix will keep the house going until you decide what you want.

I want you to try for me, but I also want you to stay there for you. I miss you. I love you. Please don't let us hold you back from living the most amazing life possible. We are so proud of you and love you so much.

Go start a new life.

Love you to the moon and back,

Mom

I LET THE LETTER FALL TO MY CHEST AS THE TEARS GUSH DOWN my face. I don't know what to think or even do, for that matter. How do I leave everything I know behind and start over in a place I have no clue about? How do I go and live with someone whom I have never met? She is asking way too much of me, but I know she is right.

So with a heavy sigh, I roll over to my side. My gaze falls on a picture of my father and mother in a tight embrace, both smiling as they look into each other's eyes. Reaching out, I take the frame in my hand, bringing it in close to my chest against the letter, the money, and the ticket to my new life. As sobs pour out of me, I whisper, "Why did you guys have to leave me?"

A NOTE FROM TONI ALEO

Thank you so much for joining me in Spring Grove!!! I hope you had a great time and didn't get too drunk...unlike poor Gen. Girl can't hold her liquor. ;-)

As always, thank you to my amazing beta team, all of whom always tell me how it is and do their best to steer me right. Thanks to Lisa Holletta (whose name I refuse to spell correctly) who makes sure I always make my deadlines. Thank you to my family and my puppy Gaston, who always do everything in their power to keep me from making those deadlines... Good thing I love them

Hope you enjoyed Not the One. I hope to make a trip back to Spring Grove soon...

Love,

Toni

(Paranormal)

Pieces

Broken Pieces

Spring Grove Novels

(Small-town romances)

Not the One

Small-Town Sweetheart

Standalones

Let it be Me

Two-Man Advantage

Misadventures

(Standalones)

Misadventures with a Rookie

Misadventures of a Manny

Assassins Series

Taking Shots

Trying to Score

Empty Net

Falling for the Backup

Blue Lines

About the
AUTHOR

My name is Toni Aleo, and I'm a #PredHead, #sherrio, #potterhead, and part of the #familybusiness!
I am also a wife to my amazing husband, mother of a gamer and a gymnast, and also a fur momma to Gaston el Papillion.
While my beautiful and amazing Shea Weber has been traded from my Predators, I'm still a huge fan. But when I'm not cheering for him, I'm hollering for the whole Nashville Predators since I'll never give my heart to one player again.
When I'm not in the gym getting swole, I'm usually writing, trying to make my dreams a reality, or being a taxi for my kids.

I'm obsessed with Harry Potter, Supernatural, Disney, and anything that sparkles! I'm pretty sure I was Belle in a past life, and if I could be on any show, it would be Supernatural so I could hunt with Sam and Dean.
Also, I did mention I love hockey, right?

Also make sure to join the mailing list for up to date news from Toni Aleo:
JOIN NOW!

www.tonialeo.com
toni@tonialeo.com

CPSIA information can be obtained
at www.ICGtesting.com
Printed in the USA
LVHW041527031119
636187LV00001B/203/P